Rawhiti Island Medics

Welcome to Rawhiti Island!

Sparks are set to fly with the arrival of new GP single dad Owen—especially when he meets widow Carly. She's only on the island for a few more weeks, but she's promised to show him *everything* island life has to offer… Meanwhile, nurse Mia is navigating the challenges of being a single mom—and she's doing fine, honest! But when her little one's father lands back in her life, she faces her biggest challenge yet: telling him he has a daughter! Carly and Mia have put the idea of finding love behind them, but what will they do when it lands on their doorstep?

Meet the Rawhiti Island Medics with…
Resisting the Single Dad Next Door

And dive into Mia's story in
Reunited by the Nurse's Secret

Both available now!

Dear Reader,

I'm so lucky to call beautiful Auckland, New Zealand, my home. The water off the east coast—the Hauraki Gulf—has around fifty islands, some large and inhabited and some just islets barely above sea level. It is here where I placed the fictional island of Rawhiti, very reminiscent of another island that we visit every year with family and friends. The Mansion House, the camp and the little penguins really do exist.

Rawhiti has always been Mia's home. It's where she draws solace after the tragedy that took her family and where she still lives with her precious little girl. So when her daughter's father, Brin, arrives on the island one stormy night, Mia's life is thrown into turmoil. Brin's too, because he wasn't aware he had a daughter!

I loved writing this book, trying to help these two work out their issues and watch them fight their growing attraction…unsuccessfully! And I love how they both focus on what's important for their little girl, putting her needs first.

I hope you enjoy *Reunited by the Nurse's Secret*. Thank you for taking a chance on one of my books. Catch up with my news at louisageorge.com.

Happy reading!

Louisa xxx

REUNITED BY THE NURSE'S SECRET

LOUISA GEORGE

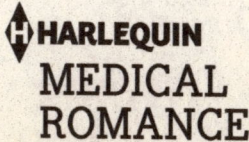

HARLEQUIN

MEDICAL
ROMANCE

HARLEQUIN®
MEDICAL
ROMANCE™

Recycling programs
for this product may
not exist in your area.

ISBN-13: 978-1-335-59514-0

Reunited by the Nurse's Secret

Copyright © 2023 by Louisa George

Harlequin Enterprises ULC
22 Adelaide St. West, 41st Floor
Toronto, Ontario M5H 4E3, Canada
www.Harlequin.com

Printed in U.S.A.

Award-winning author **Louisa George** has been an avid reader her whole life. In between chapters, she's managed to train as a nurse, marry her doctor hero and have two sons. Now she writes chapters of her own in the medical romance, contemporary romance and women's fiction genres. Louisa's books have variously been nominated for the coveted RITA® Award and the New Zealand Koru Award, and have been translated into twelve languages. She lives in Auckland, New Zealand.

Books by Louisa George

Harlequin Medical Romance

A Sydney Central Reunion
Ivy's Fling with the Surgeon

Rawhiti Island Medics
Resisting the Single Dad Next Door

Royal Christmas at Seattle General
The Princess's Christmas Baby

A Puppy and a Christmas Proposal
Nurse's One-Night Baby Surprise
ER Doc to Mistletoe Bride
Cornish Reunion with the Heart Doctor

Visit the Author Profile page
at Harlequin.com for more titles.

Praise for
Louisa George

"A single dad, an unexpected pregnancy, secret crush, friends to lovers, Louisa George combines so many of my favourite tropes in her latest outing to Oakdale... This series is right up there with Sarah Morgan's medical romances...and it's no secret how much I love those."

—*Goodreads* on *Nurse's One-Night Baby Surprise*

PROLOGUE

As LEAVING DOS WENT, this one was a disaster. Not because no one had come, but because *everyone* was here, from his direct boss and shift colleagues to the admin staff, the call receivers and the boss's boss's boss.

Either they were all sad to see him go or it was just a good excuse for a booze-up. Either way, the bar was heaving, the chatter and laughter closing in on him. It always happened: that sense of disconnection, of being an observer rather than part of it all. As if he were floating out of his body and looking down on himself, sitting at a table on the first floor of a crowded bar, overlooking Auckland's Viaduct basin out onto a marina full of very expensive yachts, hemmed in by people he'd likely never see again.

He'd clearly had too much of the delicious craft beer they sold here. Time to make a discreet exit.

He went to stand but Lewis, his boss—senior Intensive Care paramedic—and good friend, clapped him on the back. He was swaying and his eyes looked unfocused—another victim of the craft-beer allure. 'Brin, my mate. Are you sure we can't convince you to stay?'

Brin laughed. 'Ah. If you could have a word with Immigration and get them to magic me a new visa, that would be amazing. I love New Zealand.'

'Not enough to commit to a permanent job, though? They won't issue a visa on a temporary contract.'

But that was all Brin was prepared to sign up for. He shrugged; he had his reasons to keep on moving. 'I might come back—you never know. I just need to see a bit more of this side of the world first.'

'Australia's lucky to have you. But there's always a job for you here.'

'Cheers, mate. Thanks.' Brin squeezed out of his seat and indicated he was heading to the loo. But, once out of eyeshot of the crowd, he swerved left, took the escalator to the ground floor and walked out into the pedestrianised area filled with bars, restaurants and hotels, where he took a deep breath and slowly let it out.

He wasn't big on goodbyes. Had anyone noticed? He glanced up to the first floor, where laughter floated a decibel above a regular bass beat. No. He stuck his hands in his pockets, still looking up at the bar, double-checking for anyone noticing his departure, and strode towards his fancy hotel—a treat for his last night in the country.

The first thwack hit his gut.

The second took out his right hip.

What the hell?

Fists clenched, he whirled round one-eighty degrees, but there was no apparent assailant. He hauled in a breath.

God, that hurt his belly.

Then he heard a groan. A woman was sprawled on the ground in front of him. She must have tripped and grabbed him as she slid to the ground. She was wearing a sparkly silver dress and some seriously sexy stilettos.

And noticing them was entirely inappropriate. He squatted down to make eye contact. 'Hey. Are you okay? God, I'm sorry. I wasn't looking—'

'Sorry, I wasn't looking.'

They both spoke at the same time.

'Well, that'll teach us.' He quickly assessed her. She didn't seem injured, just a little stunned. Clearly, she hadn't had the wind knocked out of her, as he had. 'Yell out if anything hurts.'

'Only my ego.' She looked up at him, all big brown eyes and amazing mouth, silky with red lipstick. Then she shifted position to sit on the ground and check her legs. 'But if I was wearing tights they'd be ruined.'

Which drew his eyes to her legs: good legs, a great body and pretty face. She had the kind of tan that came from being outdoors, not a bottle, a cloud of blonde curls and soft, large brown eyes.

Then she glanced behind her, the way he'd done a moment ago, as if checking she wasn't being followed.

His sore gut squeezed. 'Hey, are you in some kind of danger?'

'Of being caught leaving a thirtieth birthday party at the crucial tequila-shots-and-dancing-on-the-tables-stage…?' She laughed and something about the sweet sound was a balm to his heart. She put up her hands. 'Guilty as charged.'

'Aw, that's the best bit. *Dancing Queen* on repeat.'

'Over there.' She pointed to a nearby bar displaying a *Private Party* sign outside. 'Feel free. I doubt anyone would mind.'

'No thanks. To be honest, I'm escaping too.'

'Oh? Tell me everything.' She undid her sandal straps and slid them off her feet, then stuck out her hand, which he took as a sign to help her stand. Which he did. As he levered her up, he noted a few things: she was light as air; her scent, with a hint of jasmine and sea salt, wrapped around him and made him think of warm summer nights; she was entirely happy to walk barefoot—a real New Zealand thing, he'd learnt; and she wasn't wearing a wedding ring.

She walked to the marina railing, leant against it, took a deep breath and let it out very slowly, as if she was trying to calm herself. All thoughts of telling her why he was running away from…well, life…disappeared. 'You sure you're not hurt?'

'Sure.' She nodded. 'Where's your accent from?'

'Ireland.'

'Ah. I couldn't decide if you were Scottish or Irish.'

'Like me and the Kiwi and Australian accents. I always get them mixed up. And probably cause offence in the process.'

'Too right.' She gaped at him. 'We sound nothing alike.'

'You sound exactly alike. But I'm heading to Australia tomorrow, so maybe I'll notice the difference when I'm there.'

Her head tilted to one side as she looked at him. 'You're leaving? Tomorrow?'

'Aye. Australia for a four-month contract. Then…who knows? Maybe Asia or South America.'

Her eyes narrowed. 'What are you running from, Mr Irish?'

Ah, yes. That. 'Brin. Sure, you don't want to know.'

Her smile was all kinds of seductive. 'Oh, I really do, Brin.'

'Seriously, the less you know about me, the better. What's your name?'

She turned to look out at the boats. 'Mi... chelle.'

He wasn't sure if she'd hesitated or hiccupped. And he also wasn't sure if she was telling him the truth. Or maybe that was just the way they pronounced 'Michelle' around here. 'Well, Mi... chelle, nice to meet you.'

She took his hand and looked up at him. 'You too, Brin the Irish man.' The way she said his name made his chest heat and his skin fizz.

'Will you be okay getting home or can I help you...?'

Her face brightened. 'I'm not going home.'

'No? A real runaway, then.'

'I'm staying there.' She pointed towards *his* hotel. 'My friend treated me to a night of luxury. I don't get the chance to come to the city very often.'

Was it a coincidence that they were staying at the same hotel? He wasn't sure he believed in coincidences, or fate. Was she staying there alone? Was she single? 'Because of your family?'

That seemed a good way of finding out the answers to his questions.

She whirled round, eyes suddenly guarded. 'What?'

Oh, he'd touched a nerve there. He backtracked a little, not wanting to upset her more. Up to now, and discounting the bruised gut, this had been a fine encounter and he was having fun. 'You don't visit the city often…because you have a brood of kids and a husband you adore, somewhere rural?'

To be fair, she looked far too young to have a brood. Maybe one or two.

A family? As if he knew what that was. If he'd touched anyone's nerve, it was his own.

'Somewhere rural? Kind of.' She nodded. 'No kids. No husband. No…' She suddenly looked bone-tired and very, very sad. She pressed her lips together and stared back out to sea. He wondered why she was so sad and if there was anything he could do to help her.

Then he wondered why he was even thinking that. He'd just met her. She was a stranger—a beautiful stranger. And he was leaving in the morning. So, he had nothing to lose, right?

'Hey. Sorry if I said something wrong.' He reached out and touched her shoulder. Was that too much? Could he touch her? Was that okay? Probably not; he took his hand away.

She looked at him, eyes swimming with unshed tears, and his heart kind of folded in on itself. She looked lost as she said, 'No. No, nothing at all. I'm just…ah…you know. Probably drank too much wine. I shouldn't. It makes me depressed.'

'I get that. Best not to have too much. That's why I was running away too. People kept buying me farewell drinks, and it's rude not to take them, but then I get drunk and I think about things I shouldn't…' Images of what he'd left back in Ireland swam in his head. He forced them away.

'Two runaways.' She touched his arm and brought him back to the present, which was a hell of a lot prettier than his past. So now he'd touched her, and she'd touched him, and he felt a whole lot better about everything. Her eyes were still misted but there was something else there—a glimmer of mischief—and he liked that. A lot.

She smiled. 'We could probably get into a whole lot of trouble.'

'If we're lucky,' he quipped.

Her eyes widened in response. 'I don't believe in luck. But I do believe in getting into the right kind of trouble.'

Oh, God.

She was seriously something. In another life he might have made a move on her. But he was getting on that plane tomorrow and she looked like the kind of woman who'd want more. Who *deserved* more. More than he could give for sure.

But, just in case, so as to not misread her context, he asked, 'What kind of trouble, exactly?'

She leaned closer. 'I'm not sure yet. But I guess if we're both here in the city for one night and we literally bump into each other and we're both on the run…' She smiled, slow and tantalising. 'There must be a reason. Something's brought us together. I mean, I never come to town, and this is your last night here. So why did we meet tonight? Why you? Why me? Why here? Why now?'

'I've no idea.' He shrugged. 'Coincidence? Fate?'

'Fate?' She giggled. 'You believe in all that?'

'That a higher force has brought us to this spot, this moment?' Nah, he didn't believe that. And yet, she did have a point.

She shrugged and giggled. 'It would be a shame not to honour the Fates if they do exist, though. Or we might incur their wrath.'

He chuckled. As come-on lines went, this was right up there. 'Yeah, best not annoy the Fates. What do you think they have in mind for us, Mi…chelle?'

'I don't know.' She drummed her fingers against her bottom lip. 'I'm just trying to decide…'

'Anything I can do to help crystallise your ideas, let me know.'

She edged closer, close enough for him to see the smattering of freckles over her nose, the layer of mascara on long, thick eyelashes and the quick dart of her tongue across her lips before she said, 'Talk with me, Brin.'

Talk? That was out of left field.

'Sure. About what?'

'I don't care. I just like listening to your accent. It takes me away from…' She shivered, clearing her throat, as if trying to clear her head too. 'It's lyrical and soft and so different to what I'm used to. I like the way you sound.'

Oh, hell.

His body prickled as his libido sprang fully into life. 'To be honest, I like the way you... everything.'

He had to admit feeling intrigued as to what exactly the sound of his voice was taking her away from.

'That makes two of us.' She put her hand on his chest and stepped closer. 'So, tell me something—anything. Just keep talking...and we'll see where we end up.'

CHAPTER ONE

Three years later...

THE ROAR OF helicopter blades as they flew across the tempestuous Hauraki Gulf just about smothered the raging clatter of Mia's heart and the rush of panic whistling through her head.

It had all happened so fast. One minute she'd been celebrating the sale of her late parents' property—an outdoors education camp—which had made her, if not exactly rich, then financially comfortable. She'd been raising a glass and planning a night of partying in Auckland city before waving her best friend off on an exciting adventure. The next minute, they'd received news so terrifying her legs had almost buckled beneath her.

Her beloved home, Rāwhiti Island, twenty-two kilometres off the Auckland coast, was suffering an ugly storm and a passenger ferry had capsized in one of the bays—a ferry no doubt carrying people she knew and loved who could be in danger. The storms could be cruel here, Mia knew to her cost. Roofs got blown off, trees felled and power cut.

People died.

Her daughter, Harper, was on the island too. The beautiful little girl who had, if not saved Mia's life, then given her something to live for. So, she wouldn't be able to breathe properly until she had Harper safely in her arms. She'd decided to return immediately. Mia wasn't about to lose anyone else.

But there was more…so much more she could barely believe.

As she climbed into the rescue chopper to go back and help her island *whanau*—her family, not by blood but by choice—she found the space occupied by two guys in green paramedic uniforms. Their faces were half-obscured by baseball caps and the chopper headsets. One of them, though, was unmistakable: tall with short, black hair… and startling navy-blue eyes.

Her past caught up with her as her heart stuttered and her gut clenched.

Why now? Why today of all days? Why this helicopter, at this exact moment, on this day?

The guy sitting opposite her was an Irishman called Brin. Clearly a paramedic, although he hadn't told her that when they'd met three years ago. And, judging by the way he was looking at her, he was just as blindsided seeing her again as she was seeing him. His shocked gaze caught hers as the chopper juddered roughly through grey clouds. A crosswind dumped them a few metres down towards the sea. Mia yelped as the skipper wrestled with the controls. Would they even survive this flight?

Next to her, her best friend and sister-in-law, Carly, squeezed her hand.

Mia tore her eyes away from Brin, still trying to reconcile the fact he was here and wondering where to start, what to say. How to explain…?

'Hey, it's going to be okay,' Carly mouthed over the din.

'I don't think so.' She shrugged at her friend. She was not okay at all. She wasn't ready for this, neither her head nor her heart. Not amongst the turmoil of a rescue and God knew what else they'd be facing on Rāwhiti.

'Prepare for a bumpy landing,' the skipper's voice crackled through her headset.

She gripped Carly's hand, then they were descending fast through lumps and bumps that buffeted them like a washing machine spin-cycle. Carly's face was pale. Brin was steadfastly looking out the front window into the darkness.

'Welcome to Rāwhiti.' The skipper chuckled. 'Good luck out there.'

Then the door hatch opened. Mia took off her headset, unclipped her safety buckle and was bundled out into a wind that hit her in the chest and whipped most of her breath away. The skipper shoved their suitcases into their arms...so excitedly packed and sadly unused...and they ran out of chopper-blade range to be met by one of the locals, Nikau.

He took her bag and shouted, 'Carly, Mia, thank God you're here. Everyone's evacuated to the camp and the injured are being taken there too.'

Carly nodded and raced ahead. Having been the island's first responder, she no doubt wanted to get into the thick of the rescue efforts. Mia supposed she should tell the paramedics where they were headed but they just followed Carly. Mia trailed behind, descending the steep path towards the back of the outdoor education camp—the place she had just sold.

Chaos...in her head, in her body, here at the camp. Rain lashed the windows and wind rattled the window frames as people bustled around the huge kitchen-dining room, trying to dry off or attend to the injured. Added to the battering wind and rain were the raised voices of people in pain, people who were frightened, people at risk.

She ran from group to group, trying to find Harper, then stumbled outside into the downpour, only to have a woman with a nasty gash on her forehead thrust at her.

There was no time to think, so Mia helped the woman to the makeshift minor-injury assessment area in a cordoned-off area of the room.

She'd left Harper in the care of Owen, the island doctor, and his four-year-old son, Mason. Owen would not have let anything happen to them. They wouldn't have been on the ferry. They were safe; she was sure.

But, hell, how many times had she told herself that that terrible night when her parents and brother hadn't come home?

They are safe. How many times had she repeated those words for the next week until reality had crashed in? How many hours had she and Carly sat together, hoping, wishing, praying for their family to return? And then no one had. Mia had been left without her parents and brother, Rafferty. Carly had been made a widow. All they'd had left was each other, and Harper had cemented the bond: mother, auntie, baby.

Mia pulled herself together. She was sure her baby was okay…but where was she?

'Have you got any painkillers?' The woman in front of her moaned and Mia forced herself to focus on her job. She was the island nurse-practitioner. Everyone depended on her to stay focused and calm. She grabbed a first-aid kit, explained to her patient what she was going to do and made sure the woman had no other injuries she needed to deal with.

And, always, she was aware of the feeling she was being watched. She turned her head and saw Brin kneeling on the floor, attending to a boy who looked around nine years old. Not a local kid. As if he felt her eyes on him, Brin turned and looked at her. His expression was one of confusion, his eyes narrowed as if he was trying to get a better look at her.

She looked away and focused on cleaning the head wound.

Not here. Not now.

When? How? Why? What the hell was she going to say?

Because, now he was here in front of her, she had to tell him.

He said something to the boy's mum then stood.

Was he coming over? What was he going to say?

She didn't want to hear him speak. That cute Irish accent had been the undoing of her three years ago. He'd seduced her with his words. Hell, she'd been putty in his hands. But the ramifications of where that voice had taken her, what they'd done that night, were still rippling and would do so for the rest of Mia's life.

Her heart thumped in time with each of his steps as he strode towards her.

'Mia! You're here! Thank God.' Anahera, Mia's friend and receptionist at Mia's workplace, Rāwhiti Medical Clinic, slid in front of Brin and wrapped her in a hug. Over her friend's shoulder, she watched Brin pause and frown.

Mia. Hell—he'd heard. No matter; she had more immediate things to worry about. She grasped Anahera's shoulders. 'Where's Harper?'

Anahera stroked Mia's arm. 'Breathe, Mia. Breathe. Don't worry, hon. She's fast asleep in one of the bunk rooms upstairs. Nicole's in there, and her babies too. I just left them to come down here to help out. I'm so glad you came home. Is Carly...? Did she go?'

Having lost her husband, and too afraid to let herself fall in love with Owen, Carly had booked a one-way ticket around the world, planning to leave the country tomorrow. But, as she and Mia had celebrated the camp sale and contemplated their futures, Carly had realised she loved Owen and had come back to see if he felt the same about her. 'She's come home too, but I don't know where she is now. We jumped off the helicopter and she disappeared in a huge rush.'

'Probably gone to find Owen. He's co-ordinating the rescue in North Bay.'

'Right. Yes. Good. They'll need all the help they can to rescue the boat passengers.'

'Poor guy's first emergency on his own. Well... I guess he has Carly now too.' Anahera smiled.

'Oh, I think he has.' Mia forced a smile of her own. At least one good thing was coming out of this fated night. Carly and Owen's relationship had stalled when she'd decided to head overseas but now Mia could only hope they'd get back on track. But this night, the storm and these injuries, would bring back fearful memories for Carly too.

Anahera nodded. 'That's something, then. Little Mason's in the bunk room upstairs too.'

All her loved ones were accounted for. Mia did what Anahera had asked and finally breathed out. *Good. Right, focus, Mia.*

'I've set up a major injury space in the accessible room down the corridor and the walking wounded are over there.' Anahera pointed towards Brin. 'I don't know what we'll do when this place changes hands. Nowhere on the island has this kind of space.'

Mia grimaced. She and Carly had signed the sale and purchase agreement only hours ago, although it felt like a lifetime. This place was no longer hers and she had no idea what it might turn into. The last rumour had been about a fancy upmarket resort.

Guilt worried down her spine as she looked around the familiar room used by generations of school children to learn bush skills and sailing. Memories came of her parents teaching those skills: the love they'd had for their jobs; her brother joining the teaching team as he'd grown older. Then Carly marrying him and coming to live here five years ago.

So many memories were imprinted on these walls. Her whole life until eighteen had been lived here…then three years away at nursing college and subsequent years in a little cottage in a different part of the island. But the camp had always been her home. Until a perfect storm of issues—Carly leaving and not being able to find a replacement; much-needed renovation they'd been unable to afford; and Mia's own little cottage requiring some serious TLC—had collided and they'd decided to sell Camp Rāwhiti.

But had she made a mistake by selling? Had she betrayed her family's memory? No. She couldn't think about that right now.

'Mia!' Nikau was standing in the doorway, his arm wrapped around the waist of a man who was hopping on one foot.

Mia glanced at Brin. He stared back at her, then turned away.

I can explain...

Mia's heart jerked as she watched him stride to the door, his back rigid as he nodded at Nikau, then head towards the high-need assessment area.

A peal of thunder roared above them, shaking the windows. The sky lit up with a flash of bright white. Someone screamed. A baby started to cry. Noise filled her ears, her chest.

And suddenly she did want to hear Brin's voice, to have his soothing words whispered against her neck.

'It's okay. It's okay. You are beautiful. You are amazing. I want you. You feel... God, you feel so good. I'm so glad I found you. It's okay. It's okay.

It's okay…' he'd said as she'd blubbed against his chest, overwhelmed by so much emotion from the singular act of love-making. As she'd lost herself in sensory overload with this smooth-talking man, his mind-melting kisses, his heat. Had sought pleasure, given pleasure, unburdened herself of six months' worth of grief in touch, feel and sensation.

Then he'd made her laugh with stupid jokes and they'd talked about…what? Books, movies, travel, likes, dislikes, other things… But not everything. She hadn't told him her real name, where she lived and what she did because it hadn't seemed important. They'd only had one night, after all. But she had talked about her hopes and her dreams. It had been liberating to be effervescent, carefree Michelle instead of tragic Mia.

Right now, she ached to feel as unburdened and free as she had that night. To have him hold her again. To feel less alone. To explore *him* again. To relive every delicious second…and maybe even tell him the truth, at least about her name.

But she had so much truth to tell him she didn't know how to begin.

Mia?

Brin walked away from the woman he'd thought was Michelle. Was it her? He was sure of it. She had the same halo of blonde curls; the dark, soulful eyes. But his Michelle…*his*? What the hell? He gave a rueful laugh, then corrected himself. The woman he'd spent the night with would have shown some sort of recognition other than aversion and avoidance, surely? It had been one of the most memorable nights of his life. The connection had been instant, the attraction off the scale. But had it been more than just great sex?

Yeah, he'd thought so. Hell, he'd almost considered staying in Auckland just to spend more time with her, but with his visa expiring the next day he hadn't been able to take the risk. They'd agreed not to swap contact details. The mystery had amped up the sex appeal and he'd preferred to keep his heart intact by not investing too deeply or too much.

Besides, he'd left his tattered roots in Ireland. He wasn't about to start putting any down in this tiny country at the end of the world.

He trawled through possible scenarios. Maybe she had an identical twin, and this was indeed that twin called Mia. Maybe Michelle had had a reason to lie to him—perhaps she had had a husband and a brood of kids. Perhaps she was scared he might blurt out what they'd done in front of everyone here and put her in a difficult situation. Surely, she'd think better of him than that?

Truth was, he couldn't second-guess what any woman was thinking these days, if his failed marriage and the lies that were embroidered through it were anything to go by.

The major assessment space was empty, which he knew could only be a good thing. They'd been told to expect serious casualties, but the rescue team had clearly done a great job of getting the ferry passengers to safety without too much physical trauma. Although, the emotional trauma of being on a sinking boat in the dark and a raging storm would probably last longer.

But out here he could breathe for a moment, get his head round seeing this woman again before heading back in and working with her. When she'd stepped on to the helicopter and their eyes had met, he'd wanted to grin and wrap her in his arms. But the guarded way she'd looked at him had given him a very strong message of rebuttal, even denial.

A high-pitched wail had him turning round to find a woman holding a crying toddler. A girl, around two years old, maybe a little more. She was a mess of black curls, with pale skin and sleepy blue eyes. She rubbed the silky border of a well-worn blanket between her fingers. Cute kid...but obviously very upset. Then the blanket floated to the ground and the wailing intensified. Brin picked it up and handed it back to her.

'Hey, you don't want to lose your blankie. I know it's precious. I had one just like it when I was your age.'

Funny; he'd forgotten until this minute.

Fat tears dotted her cheeks and her chest juddered as she breathed in, telling him she'd been crying for a while. She held the blanket close to her chest and stared at him. But he laughed at her possessiveness. 'Don't worry, *mo stór*. I won't take it away from you.'

'Blankie.' She stared at him, and he wondered if she was warning him not to touch it or just repeating the word.

'Yes, blankie.' Suddenly desperate to see her smile, he flicked the bottom of the blanket over her head. 'Oh? Where's she gone? Where is she?'

A sniff.

'Where's she gone?' he tried again.

A gurgle.

Then she pulled the blanket down and giggled. Someone had taught her hide-and-seek.

He flicked it up again to cover her face. 'She's gone again. Where is she?'

The giggle became a full belly-laugh as she tugged the comforter away from her face. The tears were gone. And, oh, those huge dark-blue eyes and that messy hair, a tangle of black…kind of like his had been before he'd had it cut. The sullen pout that had transformed into the prettiest smile he'd ever seen was too cute.

There was something about her that made his chest feel warm.

Mo stór. My darling.

How many times had he said that? His heart suddenly ached for the little girl he'd left behind in Ireland. She was a few years older than this one, but he remembered the toddler stage all too well: the tantrums and the cuteness overload, the beginnings of a real personality. She'd been like him, he'd thought—a dreamer and a pleaser. Funny, too, just like him.

Yeah. Not so funny now.

He rubbed at his chest and the little girl started to cry again.

'It's okay, Harper. It's okay. Let's see if we can find your mammy in the dining room.' The woman flashed Brin a weary smile and bustled past him. He held the door open and let her through.

As he followed her into the noisy room, his eyes immediately and instinctively found Michelle again. She was crouched on her haunches, taking an elderly man's blood pressure. The old man was wrapped in a foil blanket and even from here Brin could see him shivering. But Michelle was tender and reassuring…he knew because he'd seen her in action earlier. She was assured in her medical skills, and compassionate. A nurse—he hadn't even known that.

The woman with the girl walked over to Michelle and handed her the crying toddler. Michelle's face creased into a grin, then crumpled into a grimace as she started to cry too. She wrapped the child in her arms, rocking her back and forth.

He remembered the way Michelle had cried in his arms that night, the breathless sobs she'd said were from making love with him. From being touched after a long time. From giving and taking pleasure, the overwhelm of their attraction. But he'd sensed there'd been more to it as she'd gripped him and her tears had soaked his chest.

And he'd been right.

Michelle had been on the chopper and had a small suitcase. How long had she been away?

And was she the little girl's mother?

Clearly this was her reason not to have told him the truth about her home life. She *did* have a family.

Hell. One thing he really hated was lying—lying where children were involved, in particular.

'Brin. Can you give me a hand?' Lewis, his old and new colleague, called over to him and gestured towards a woman with a badly misshapen leg. 'Going to need your silky skills for this one.'

'On it.' Brin shook away the emotion he thought he'd got a handle on and threw himself back into his work.

At least that was something he could rely on.

CHAPTER TWO

IT FELT AS if the stream of injuries was never going to end, but as the last of the passengers, the boat skipper, Carly, Owen and the rescue team all piled into the dining room, things started to calm down. Everyone had been safely rescued, but the boat was sinking.

At least the casualties were relatively minor, save for a couple of patients who needed fairly quick evacuation to Auckland General Hospital, which Lewis was trying to organise, but he kept getting rebutted because of the downturn in the weather.

Mia had managed to get Harper to go back upstairs with Nicole and she hadn't heard a peep from her since. And, yes, she knew Brin had seen her with her daughter. She hadn't dared look at him, so had no idea what he might be thinking.

This was all such a mess. Her thoughts and emotions were all over the place. She'd cried, holding Harper, in front of all those people. Her guard had dropped, she'd felt so protective, he was here and…oh, God. Her heart felt as if it were going to hammer out of her chest. Did he know? Had he guessed?

A steaming mug of hot chocolate was pushed into her hands. Carly smiled at her. 'You've done a great job with all these patients. Drink this. It'll keep your strength up.'

'Thanks.' Mia took the cup and noticed her hands were trembling.

It seemed as though Carly had noticed too. 'Can I say, you look terrible, Mia. Are you okay?'

'Thanks muchly. You don't look so great yourself,' Mia threw back, laughing. Carly was soaked to the skin, hair plastered to her face, and sporting a tinfoil blanket. But she was bright and cheery and had a very secretive smile every time she looked over at Owen.

'I'm going for a shower as soon as I get the chance,' Carly said. 'Do you want to go upstairs for a while to be with Harper?'

'I need to stay here in case we have any further medical problems.' Plus, she wanted to make sure Brin got on that chopper soon and headed off the island.

'There are enough of us to cope without you,' her friend said.

'No. I'm fine.' Mia realised she'd snapped. 'I'm sorry. I'm—'

'Hey, it's okay.' Carly smiled softly. 'This must be bringing up all kinds of emotions for you. I

know it did for me. I just had a bit of a wobble
out there on the boat with Owen.'

Her friend didn't know the half of it. Mia
shrugged. 'I'll be okay. What about you? What
kind of wobble?'

'I had a meltdown when I thought there might
be some people left on the ferry and were going
to drown. I screamed a bit and there were tears as
the memories piled in. But Owen got me through.
And no one died.' Carly wrapped her in a hug,
avoiding spilling the hot chocolate. 'I'm okay.
But tell me what you need, Mia. If you want to
go hug your girl, then go. If you need a shower,
go right ahead. Some quiet time? I can muster a
room for you upstairs.'

'Gosh, where would I be without you?' Mia
hugged her friend, trying not to cry. 'I'm so glad
you decided to stay.'

'Me too. I was overwhelmed by the feelings I'd
grown for Owen and I panicked and wanted to
run away. But, as soon as I left this island, I knew
I'd made a mistake.' Carly squeezed Mia tightly.
'After Rafferty died, I didn't want to fall in love
and then risk losing it all again. And I didn't want
you to think I'd ever forget him.'

'I know you won't ever forget my brother. But
I also know you love Owen, and you need to cel-
ebrate it. Wallow in it.'

'Oh, I will.' Carly's eyes crinkled. 'So, what
do you need, Mia?'

I want to rewind to that night in the hotel.

The thought almost brought her to her knees: comfort; peace; exhilaration; being held. Finding pleasure that had wiped away some of her grief, if only for a few hours. For that, she'd been eternally grateful. And there'd been that ethereal… *something* between them. Something she'd never forgotten and had never found with any other man since. Not that there'd been any who had got past the first-date stage.

It had been a bone-deep connection. *A knowing.* An understanding she couldn't even begin to describe. But then, it had been laced through with her lies, so maybe she was just looking back with rose-coloured glasses.

She extricated herself from Carly's hug and forced another smile. 'I'm good. Honestly. I've already had a big hug with Harper. She needs to sleep now, or it'll be Miss Grumpy Pants tomorrow, and I really don't have the energy to deal with that.'

'Okay, if you're sure.' Carly was looking at her with a puzzled expression which Mia was not going to solve for her any time soon. She'd spent the last three years avoiding any discussion about Harper's parentage and wasn't about to start talking now. Not here. Not ever, if possible.

But it wasn't going to be possible; she knew that now. He was back. 'I'm sure.'

Her friend sighed. 'Okay. Well, I've just heard

that the weather's too bad for the paramedics to evacuate the tibial fracture and the collarbone injury in the short term. So, we need to make up a room for them to rest in. Owen was hoping that between you, him and the two paramedics you could do a roster, to take it in turns to get a break while the others monitor the patients.'

Which might mean she would spend more time with Brin. Mia shuddered. 'Sure.'

'Great. I'll sort out a room in the annexe with bedding, if you could take this tray of drinks over to the guys?' Carly pointed to a tray on the table next to her and then flitted towards the exit.

'The guys' meaning Brin and the senior paramedic, Lewis, who was a regular on the medical evacs. Taking the drinks meant she'd have to look Brin in the eye, which she'd so far managed to avoid, but there wasn't anything she could do about it now. So, she picked up the tray and walked towards the makeshift screen, her heart in her mouth, her stomach in knots.

As she entered the space, Brin looked up from attending a patient and caught her gaze. She tried to look away but couldn't. He was…well…just as gorgeous as he'd been that night, with searching eyes, strong jaw and a rugged, toned body— tanned now, even though he'd laughed that his Irish skin usually went bright red in the sun rather than brown.

She forced some calm into her body. 'Hey,

here's some hot chocolate.' She turned to the two patients. 'I'll check with the doc to see if you're allowed anything to eat or drink. It depends on how soon we can get you medevaced out of here. They might want you nil-by-mouth if they think we can get you to the hospital soon.'

'Might not be until tomorrow, I'm afraid. It's too wild right now.' Lewis jumped up and took the tray. 'Thanks a lot, Mia. This is great.'

She shot a look at Brin at the mention of her name. His expression was like stone. She turned back to Lewis and put as much levity into her tone as she could. 'Carly's making beds up in a bunk room in the annexe. We can take it in turns to monitor this lovely pair and then alternate getting some rest.'

'Great idea. Hey…' Lewis's expression turned serious. 'I was thinking…'

'Yes?' Mia stared up at him. He was a nice guy. Around her age, maybe a little older. Single, good-looking, outdoorsy. Not her type or anything, but she got on well with him. Maybe if she hadn't kept Brin in her heart she might have thought other men might be her type, but he'd ruined her for anyone else.

'Are you okay? I mean, this must be giving you some bad flashbacks, right?'

She briefly closed her eyes and let memories wash through her. The boat that hadn't come back. Her whole family…gone.

Then she opened them but refused to look at Brin and let him see all the emotions she carried with her. Emotions she'd wrangled into submission but were mingling with her anxiety and making her blood pressure spiral. Bereaved Mia was not bright and bubbly Michelle, although he'd probably guessed that by now. 'Yeah. It's not the best night I've ever had.'

Understatement of the year.

'I'm so sorry, Mia.' Lewis touched her arm. 'Is there anything I can do?'

'I'm okay. But thank you.' She took a deep breath. 'The best thing is for all this to be over. I'd really like the wind to die down and the sun to come out in the morning.'

'Us too. We need to get our patients to the hospital asap.' Lewis grimaced, then looked at his colleague. 'Okay. Brin, you take the first rest. Mia, would you mind showing Brin where the bunk rooms are? It's a warren up there, and especially difficult in the dark.'

No. Please, no.

'Sure.'

But Brin shook his head warily. 'I'll find it, no worries. Don't bother yourself, Mia.'

His Irish accent had the faintest Aussie tinge in it. Had he been there all this time? He'd said he was going to travel through Asia, maybe head to South America—his 'great adventure', he'd called it.

She glanced at Lewis, who was frowning as he looked first at Brin then at Mia. Then his eyes widened. 'God, sorry. Stupid of me. You two don't know each other. Mia Edwards, this is Brin O'Connor. He's our newest team member, but he's been here before. A few years ago…two?'

'Three.' Brin nodded.

'But you never came out to Rāwhiti, no?' Lewis was babbling on, totally oblivious that Brin and Mia knew each other, intimately. 'Well, this is Mia. She's our very capable nurse-practitioner here on Rāwhiti. Which is usually a gorgeous place to visit, except when it's blowing a gale.'

'Pleased to meet you… Mia.' Brin's tone was flat but this time he did look at her and his expression was guarded, confused and possibly angry.

She didn't blame him. At least he'd been honest that night. She swallowed back her anxiety. *O'Connor*—Brin O'Connor. How much easier things could have been if she'd known that little piece of information three years ago. 'Hi, Brin. Welcome to Rāwhiti.'

'Better head upstairs, mate. Time's ticking. You have an hour and counting.' Lewis tapped his watch. 'Mia, do us a favour and show him the bunk room or he'll waste all his rest time trying to find it.'

She felt the weight of everyone looking at her, so she nodded quickly then headed out of the room. If they could do this in double-quick time, she might be able to avoid awkward conversations until she was ready to answer the many questions he'd no doubt have.

Don't ask. Don't ask. Don't ask.

Once outside, there was no opportunity to talk. The wind howled and the trees bent almost sideways. The roar of the sea filled the air and the lashing rain made it undesirable to stop even for a moment. But, once inside the annexe, silence fell, weighty and laden with their history and all those unasked questions.

She ran up the steps and opened the bunk-room door, irritated to find that Carly had finished making up the beds and had obviously long gone.

She pointed to the bunks. 'There you go. Bathroom's at the far end of the corridor. Bye.' Then she turned and headed away.

'Michelle.' His voice stopped her, the way it had that night. The voice that she still dreamt of almost as often as the way he'd kissed her, held her, made love to her… They were all regular stalkers through her dreams. 'Mia. Whoever you are…'

Her heart hammered against her chest like the storm waves crashing against the rocks. She slowly turned to face him. This was it—the reckoning. 'Mia. My name's Mia, not Michelle.'

He nodded, his expression unreadable. 'I assume you had your reasons for giving me a different name.'

'I did.' It hadn't been her intention. She'd grasped a chance to be someone else for a few hours. But she needed to be honest now. She walked back into the bunk room, preferring to have this conversation out of earshot of anyone else.

He followed her inside but didn't close the door. He even stepped to one side to allow her a direct escape route. The result of training in dealing with difficult situations? Or maybe he was just giving her space.

'Is he here?' he asked.

'Who?' Mia frowned.

He sat down on one of the beds. 'Your partner—husband?'

'I don't have one.'

'Oh. I thought…' He looked at the floor. 'Okay.'

'It's…complicated.'

'Isn't it always?' His tone was sharper as he looked at her again. 'But you had one, right? Someone significant enough that you lied to me about your name, and God knows what else.'

His words stung. 'No, Brin. I'm not the kind of person who has affairs. Honestly. That's not who I am. I've never been married, and I didn't have a partner when I met you. That one night we had together? I was single. I was free to be with you.'

'So why lie about who you were?'

'I…' How to explain everything? 'Does it matter? Really?'

He huffed out a breath, stood, stalked over to the window and put his hands on the ledge, staring out into the wild night. 'It shouldn't matter, right? We both knew the score. It was a bit of harmless fun. But, yet, somehow it does. That night felt… I don't know…significant. I thought we'd connected. I was honest wit' you.'

There was his accent again, stroking her nerve endings while the emotions swirling in her chest gave the raging gale outside some serious competition. 'Really? You told me everything about your life?'

'Not everything, no. We didn't have enough time for everything.' He turned round to look at her, leaned back against the window ledge and crossed his ankles. 'It was the first time I met you. I wasn't going to bore you with my life history.'

'Exactly. So, you held things back too.' God knew, she was trying for time, absolution or… what? She didn't know.

'It was our first night,' he reiterated.

'And the last.'

'Yeah.' He held her gaze with those lovely blue eyes…eyes she looked into every day when she gazed at her daughter. But they turned dark. 'We both knew it was a one-time thing.'

'We did.' And it had been amazing, magical, life-affirming. Life-giving—literally.

He shook his head and the anger seemed to steam out of him. 'I'm sorry. I'm getting all heavy over nothing. It's okay, I get it. I was thrown by the name thing. And, to be honest, blindsided by seeing you again after all these years. It's not my business why you told me your name was Michelle.' He hesitated then huffed out a breath. 'Look, I had a bad time of it a few years back with a woman who lied to me. It messed me up for a while—makes me wary. I don't like being lied to.'

'I don't blame you.' She didn't want to think he'd been hurt before and that she had added to it. This serious Brin was another layer to add to the funny, sexy, gentle one she remembered.

'And...' He gave her a rueful smile. 'Ah, look ya. I guess I'd built up this idea of what things could have been like if we'd stayed in touch, you know? Or what our reunion might have been like.'

She'd been there too, many times, going over and over what she might say. 'Yes, me too. Didn't think it'd be like this—in a bunk room in a storm.'

'I definitely had other ideas.' His eyes briefly lit up and she wondered if his ideas featured a rerun of that night. 'But there it is.'

They both knew this conversation about wishful thinking was going nowhere so she didn't say anything else. But for a moment she allowed herself to imagine a romantic reunion where the timing and the place had been perfect. Where they'd stayed in touch, or where he hadn't left. Where she'd told him her real name and he'd told her his surname. Where she'd found him on social media. Where he'd known where she lived, or the island, at least.

Things could have been very different.

Silence filled the conversation gap and she was about to leave and try to get her head around everything. Maybe delay the important conversation to another time. Maybe…never?

But then he said, 'What did Lewis mean by "flashbacks"?'

'I'm sorry?'

'I mean…you don't have to explain, but I'm sinking here.' He ran his palm across his cropped hair and gazed at her. It dawned on her that he wasn't angry, just confused. 'I know I don't have a right to ask, Mia, but this is like a huge puzzle and I don't have a clue what's going on. Did your partner die in a storm or something? I mean…if that's what happened I don't blame you for not wanting to talk about it that night. Or…what?'

He looked lost. He thought the lie about her name was tied up in some sort of relationship tragedy. No, that was poor Carly's cross to bear. And just thinking about everything she'd lost brought Mia's barriers crashing down. 'Oh, Brin.

No, I didn't lose my partner. I lost my whole family—my mum, dad and brother. In a boating accident…before I met you. About six months or so before.'

Those navy-blue eyes darkened and he looked genuinely upset for her. Almost as if he felt her grief. 'God, Mia, that's terrible. I'm so sorry. I didn't know.'

'Why would you? That night, you said something along the lines of, "the less you know about me, the better". And I thought…yeah. Actually, let's play. It's been a long time since I played. I'd spent six months battered by grief. Everywhere I went, people looked at me with such sadness, I felt the weight of their grief piled on mine. I was exhausted and lonely. Then one of my old nursing friends invited me to a party. I really wasn't going to go but Carly, my brother's widow, pushed me into it with the lure of a luxury hotel. And I eventually caved.'

'Then you met me.'

Oh, yes. A major turning point in her life. 'We were having a good time flirting…' She paused, caught his eye and hoped to find the…something again, but it wasn't there—just bewilderment. 'I didn't want to bring all my past into our fun conversation. I wanted to be someone else. To step out of my crappy life, leave all that grief and emotion behind just for one night. Can you blame me for wanting some respite from that? My family were dead. I didn't want to be that "sole survivor" person, the one everyone pities. I wanted mysterious, exciting, sexy. Man, I just wanted to be wanted.'

He closed his eyes and she wondered what he was thinking. When he opened them again he looked at her and smiled cautiously. 'You were certainly that, Mia. I almost didn't get on the plane.'

'Because of me?' He'd thought about stalling his plans for her?

'Yeah.' He laughed. 'Crazy, eh?'

'That would have been mad.' So much had happened since. 'Did you get to do all the travelling you'd planned?'

'Some. A few months working in Aussie to boost the financials, then I got to Asia as the world went into lockdown. Bad timing, eh? I hopped on one of the last flights out of Hanoi and hunkered down back in Perth. Went straight back to the job I'd just left. My visa got extended so I stayed a while longer. Then back here.'

'Why didn't you go back home?'

He frowned. 'Home?'

'Ireland.'

He straightened and spat out, 'There's nothing for me there. Nothing at all.'

'Or stay in Perth, then? Why come back here?' Was she fishing? Was she hoping his reasons for returning were to do with her? And why such a vociferous reaction to her question?

He held up his palms. 'Lewis called me out of the blue and offered me a promotion.'

'Lewis. Of course.' All this time her friend had kept in touch with Brin and she hadn't even known. And, she noted, Brin hadn't come back to look for her—he'd come for the job opportunity. She wasn't sure she could put a name to the feelings that news instilled in her but they weren't happy ones. Damn, even now she felt intensely moved by him.

He shrugged. 'To be fair, he sounded pretty desperate, and there's a new scheme here that fast-tracks Irish paramedics. Makes getting a visa a lot easier. So why not? I like the place and the people.' He shot her a look that had her insides melting. 'It seemed like a good idea.'

'Well, you've certainly done a lot more than I have. I've just stayed here the whole time.'

'Ah, no. I wouldn't say that. In between you've had a baby. Harper, is it—your little girl? I saw you with her earlier—cute as a button.'

Oh, God.

Trepidation flooded through her, making her heart jitter and her gut tighten. She wished he'd leave, so she didn't have to tell him the truth, but that was the coward's way out. He needed to know…even if this cold, sparse room on a wild night wasn't the best time or place. The words would no doubt rock his world.

There was no easy way to say it. She felt blindsided, unprepared, even though she'd been rehearsing how and what she was going to say for almost three years. She took a breath and held his gaze.

'*Our* little girl, Brin.'

'I'm sorry?' He shook his head and took a step towards her, his eyes suddenly wild with an emotion she couldn't identify but was a lot like panic, with a flash of anger…distrust. He raised his hands, wanting answers. 'What the hell?'

'*Our* little girl.'

She swallowed. This was not the reaction she'd been hoping for. Confusion, yes—surprise, definitely—but anger, mistrust? Did he think she was lying? Trying to trap him?

But she'd gone this far, so she had to tell him the truth. 'That child is our baby, Brin. Harper is your daughter.'

CHAPTER THREE

THIS COULDN'T BE HAPPENING.

This could not freaking be happening.

Brin took a deep breath, let it out slowly and tried to control his reactions as he looked at Mia. He'd been in her presence what—three hours, four? And already his emotions were on a rollercoaster ride. She was still beautiful, guarded, soft, sexy. Oh, yes…he'd registered the physical tug towards her.

But this news?

He backed away. 'No, Mia. You've made a mistake. She's not my child.'

She blinked quickly, her tone fervent, her words coming out in a rush, as if she had so much to say and couldn't stop them. 'Yes, she is. There was no one else but you. No one. She was born thirty-seven weeks after our night.'

'But…whoa, Mia. Are you sure?'

'One hundred percent.' Her eyes widened. 'Look at her. She's got your eyes, Brin, not mine. Your fair skin. I don't know what your hair was like when you were younger, but she's certainly not inherited my blonde.'

The little girl with the blankie who'd cried then giggled and done something to his heart.

Mo stór.

That little tiny scrap of giggling prettiness was his child? He couldn't deny the hair was exactly like his at that age, the eyes blue like his, not brown like Mia's. But that was where the likeness ended, surely?

She'd been upset and he'd tried to soothe her. But why? Why not just pick up the blanket and give it to her then walk away? Why get involved?

Because there'd been something about her that had made him stop, that had called to him. Jeez, the way her mother had called to him too. Something that had made him want her to be happy, a marrow-deep, soul-deep need to protect her that had been visceral, undeniable.

If that wee girl was his child, he would love her until he died—he knew that without a doubt.

No.

No.

He wasn't going to believe her. He couldn't do that to himself again—allow himself to slide into loving a child only to have it cruelly snatched away. A pack of lies.

No.

Mia was staring at him, her lip trembling as

if she was on the verge of tears. 'Say something, Brin.'

'Like what?' He didn't trust himself to stay calm. He needed to think. He couldn't do that with her here; there was too much of her: her scent, her pretty face, the soft lilt of her voice… the tenderness. God, he remembered that—the sweet sounds she'd made when he'd slid inside her. The way she'd tasted; the swell of her breasts. Too many memories that would make him soften.

And harden.

So he left her there, in that soulless room, and walked out into the night.

Raindrops pelted his body as he wandered… to where? He didn't know where he was, save for some outdoor camp on a tiny island in the middle of a big sea. He followed the path that took him past the major-injury room, the large kitchen-dining block with condensation-covered windows and the hum of chatter, past the drying room and lecture room and out onto a flat piece of grass about the size of half a football pitch. Fifty metres or so further on he could see the large, dark shape of a building, so he headed for it. Squinting through the water running down his face, he saw a sign: *Boat Shed*. He tried the door but it was locked.

Beyond that was a small bay. The crash of waves against the pebbles assaulted him, tumultuous and messy; the squawk of birds trying to settle in a storm; the roaring wind; the groaning and rustling of trees. A child was crying somewhere inside.

His child?

His heart jerked. 'Harper.'

He tried to see how it felt to say it out loud. He didn't dislike it, it was just unfamiliar. Not a name he'd have chosen but...

But what? He'd given his first daughter an Irish name. Would he have chosen something Irish for Harper?

A daughter. Another daughter. He closed his eyes and tried to breathe, but his chest hurt, as if there was a thick weight pressing on his rib cage. He'd had no name choice to make this time, no build-up, no excitement. No going for scans or buying the cot. No birth, no firsts, just a blanket statement of fact.

A cute kid with a blankie. If she was telling the truth.

'Brin?'

Mia's voice, behind him, was tentative. He turned to see her holding a blue-and-white-striped beach towel over her head to protect herself from the rain. And as she approached his heart did a funny leap. His whole body prickled with recognition.

I see you. I know you. I remember.

No. He was not going there, not after this bombshell.

She cleared her throat as she stared up at him. 'Um… Lewis asked me to wake you. Your break finished ten minutes ago. He thinks you're still asleep.'

Hell. Had he been out here that long? He nodded, his mind a whirl of thoughts. 'Okay.'

But he didn't move. How the hell was this going to play out? What did she expect him to do, to say?

She tilted her chin up and met his gaze. There was steel in there now. The possessiveness of a mother who was not going to let her child down. 'If I'd found out I had a daughter, I'd be… Well, I'd be thrilled.'

'You sure about that? Right out of the blue? One day someone randomly throws that at you—you had no inkling, no idea? No one had thought to let you know…what, three years ago?…that this was happening?' He almost laughed at his history repeating. You'd have thought he'd have learnt his lesson by now.

But she didn't know about his past—the lies he'd been told, the love he'd given. He did not want to go there and get his heart stomped on again.

Hell, to have one woman pretend her child was his had been heart-breaking. To have a second woman do the same thing… Did he have 'mug' written across his face? Was he some sort of easy target? But it wasn't just the women he fell for, was it? His brother had been complicit too.

His *brother*. His own kin, his blood.

Betrayal ran deep and he was not going to put himself in line for that again.

And yet… Harper. That hair. That smile. That tug.

It wasn't impossible, right? The dates worked. They'd made love more than once that night. Had they used protection? He tried to remember, but knew he always did. And also knew that no contraception was one hundred percent safe.

Harper. He refused to allow her into his heart. She was cute as hell.

Mia lowered the towel and scrunched it into a ball. Rain dripped onto her top from her sodden hair. Mascara ran down her cheeks. She was impossibly pretty, even so. And pissed off at him now. She glowered. 'Well, yes, it would be a surprise, and I'm sorry there was no other way of telling you. But she's, well, she's the absolute best thing that ever happened to me.'

She didn't have to say the words; her love for her child shone from her. He'd seen the way she'd cried when she'd held Harper earlier, heard the gentle voice, seen the immediate and unstoppable smile through the tears.

'Good, Mia. I'm glad you found some happiness after what you've been through.' But that didn't mean he was going to be a pushover 'And you want what from me, exactly?'

'Nothing.' She stepped back and shook her head. 'I…don't know. I thought I should tell you.'

'Because, if I took one look at her and did the maths, I'd guess?' Because he couldn't deny there was a familial likeness. His brother had the same eyes and hair, and Niamh. His heart cleaved at the memory.

'Because you have a right to know and to see her. If you want to. And she has every right to know her father.'

He didn't reply.

She screwed the towel up tightly in her hands. Her eyes blazed and her voice raised a notch. Because she was getting angry with him or because of the howling wind? 'For God's sake, Brin, I tried to find you, but I didn't even know your surname. The hotel refused to give out any personal information, no matter how much I begged them to. I even called the bar you'd been in, but they said there hadn't been any bookings that night.'

'Ah, no, it was just an informal thing.'

She glared at him. 'You disappeared. I looked for you on social media but there was nothing.'

'I don't do any of that.' He didn't want reminders of Ireland. Of the broken relationships he'd left behind or of his brother's treachery, his ex's lies.

'Did you know that if you put *Brin from Ire-*

land into a search engine you get nearly five million hits? I went through so many of them, night after night. But I found nothing about you, so I gave up looking. Resigned myself to bringing her up on my own. I didn't know you'd come back. I didn't think I'd ever see you again.' Her eyes were wet and he wasn't sure if it was all from the rain. 'This is a shock, Brin.'

'Too right.' Seeing her again on the helicopter had been a jolt to his heart. He'd fleetingly thought…maybe? He was here again; maybe they could reconnect? But then he'd seen her reaction. She'd been scared…or wary. Or…she'd had something fundamentally important to tell him and didn't know where to begin.

But how could he untangle Mia and Harper from his ex and from the girl he'd thought was his daughter back in Ireland? How could he separate out emotions? Learn to trust that Mia was telling the truth in the aftermath of lies she'd thought were inconsequential, but had mapped out the routes they'd both taken from that night onwards?

Mia wiped the back of her hand across her face. Her clothes clung to her body, outlining contours he didn't remember. She was softer in places, thinner in others but still stunning—more so. She gave him a tentative smile. She was anxious, nervous. 'Look, I know it's a lot to take in. But if you want to… I don't know…see her, we can arrange something. I don't know what…but we should probably talk some time when we're not surrounded by chaos.'

His heart was still raging, echoing the storm that blew around them. 'Right now, the only thing I want you to arrange is a paternity test.'

'What?' Her mouth fell open.

He nodded sharply. He was not going to soften towards either of them. He was not going backwards. 'Once we get the result, then we'll know exactly where we stand.'

Without looking at her he made his way back towards the dining room. He wondered how the hell he could focus on work when his life...his whole damned life...had come crashing down.

Again.

Mia fought the hurt that swelled through her.

Not just for her but for Harper too. If there was going to be any contact between father and daughter, she'd have to be very careful Harper didn't get hurt. Brin was a traveller, a nomad, constantly moving. He didn't think of the place he grew up in as his home. Would he just as easily move on from here, from them?

Harper was his daughter. Mia had absolutely no doubt about that. He'd have to deal with it, the way she'd dealt with it the last three years.

But she'd expected him to be kinder about it. And, worse, despite everything she couldn't help feeling the pull towards him like a moth to a flame. The immediate and devastating attraction she'd felt that first night reverberated through her. Her body remembered him—his touch, his laugh, his kisses.

But she knew better now. The way he'd reacted to this news showed her he wasn't the compassionate man she remembered.

She followed him back up to the camp buildings, swatting rain from her face and tears from her eyes. She would not cry in front of him, not again. The Mia he'd known before had grown up. She was stronger now, independent, a mother. She was capable, efficient and honest.

The door flew open and Carly bounded out. 'Mia, there you are. Harper's awake and looking for...' She paused, looking at Brin then at Mia. 'Sorry, did I interrupt...?'

Mia ignored the question, her focus entirely on her daughter's well-being. 'Where is she?'

'Anahera's got her in the dining room. Don't look so worried, she's fine—just a bit tearful.'

That makes two of us.

'Thanks.'

She headed inside and straight for her daughter, but kept half an eye on Brin, who marched over to the cordoned-off area and disappeared behind the screen.

'Mumma!' Harper slipped off Anahera's knee and ran towards her, clutching her favourite and very faded yellow-and-white-checked blanket.

'Hey, cutie.' Mia whipped her daughter up into her arms and gave her neck a nuzzle. 'I missed you.'

Harper patted Mia's face. 'Ugh. Wet.'

'Yes, sweetie. It's pouring with rain out there.'

'Playground?'

Mia laughed. The camp had a little play area with a slide, a climbing frame and a little plastic blue seesaw in the shape of a whale—but who knew for how much longer, now it had been sold?

She'd never wanted to run the camp and finding people to help Carly run it had proved difficult, never mind the cost of upkeep and much-needed renovation. Plus, she was a nurse, trying to make a life for herself and her daughter on a nurse's salary. The money from the sale of her old home would give her some breathing space. Although, now Brin was back, she felt as if she couldn't get enough oxygen into her lungs.

How much easier might her life have been—*their* lives have been—if Harper's father had been around? Would she have needed to sell her parents' beloved home?

'Mumma! Playground.' Harper patted Mia's face, bringing her back to the current most pressing needs of her offspring. It was way too late to trawl through those kinds of thoughts.

She gently rubbed her daughter's head with her knuckles. 'No, darling. Not right now. It's windy and rainy and night-time. The slide will be wet and you might get blown away in the wind.'

'Please.'

'You'll get pneumonia if you go out there. No.'

'Playground.' Harper's mouth formed a pout and Mia sighed.

'Tomorrow, maybe. Once things have dried off. Not right now.'

'Playground.' Her daughter threw her blankie onto the floor.

Mia leant forward and picked it up. This was her daughter's most favourite thing in the whole world. 'Don't let it get dirty. I think it's back to bed for you, little miss. You obviously haven't had enough sleep.'

She hated saying no, but there it was—the parent's burden. Not that Brin would know. She'd been the one parenting single-handed for three years. She didn't condemn him: the poor guy hadn't known. But, now he did, would he challenge the way she'd brought up her daughter? Would he want to do things differently? Would he want joint custody? That was, if he even wanted anything to do with them when the DNA test provided the proof.

DNA test! She wanted to scream. So many questions, niggles and worries had reared their heads and pummelled this already difficult day.

Lewis appeared from behind the screen with a wheelchair. The man with the displaced collarbone sat in it upright, pale and tired. Then Brin appeared, pushing another wheelchair in which sat the woman with the broken leg. Voices crackled through their walkie-talkies and she heard something about a weather window. He was leaving.

He looked around the room and his gaze fell on Harper and her.

Mia's breath caught. This could be the last chance they had to talk, but what more was there to say? He knew where she lived now and her real name. If he wanted to get involved with his daughter, he just had to contact her. As for anything more…the one thing she'd craved ever since that wonderful night…well, that was definitely off the table. There was too much distrust now, too much space between them—three years, for a start.

But Harper wriggled off her lap and ran towards him, beaming and laughing. His gaze followed and there was a hint of reluctant amusement in his face.

Please smile.

'Blankie.' His daughter held her precious blanket out to him.

Was she offering it to him?

What? Weird.

She'd never done anything like that before to anyone. In fact, she was extremely possessive when it came to her blankie; she couldn't get to sleep without it.

How was he going to react now he knew what he knew?

'Harper, stop.' Mia would not let her daughter be hurt by this man. She jumped up and started to walk towards them. 'Harper, don't bother Brin, he's busy.'

Startled, Harper turned round and the blankie dropped to the floor.

Brin looked over at Mia then at Harper.

'No bother.' He picked up the blanket, held it out and smiled. He smiled! And it transformed his face back to the way he'd looked that night. Carefree. Gorgeous. Sexy as hell. 'Here ya go... Harper.'

Their daughter beamed at the sound of her name in his soft, lilting voice. Then she did something very strange. She put the blanket over her face.

What the heck?

Brin momentarily looked stricken then he crouched down and said something Mia couldn't catch.

Harper tugged the blanket down and giggled, then put it over her face again.

Once again, a flicker of discomfort scudded across Brin's face, then he smiled. 'Where's she gone?'

Harper pulled the blanket down and laughed again.

He patted her head and grinned, then stood, rubbed his chest and drew his eyes away from his daughter. For a beat he looked haunted, then his gaze collided with Mia's.

She'd covered the distance and was now standing in front of him. Exhaustion nipped at his features and she felt a glimmer of sympathy. He'd stayed well beyond the time his shift was supposed to finish. He was also dealing with a shock revelation.

She gently rubbed her daughter's back. 'Harper, say goodbye to Brin.'

Not Daddy, or Dad or Papa—just Brin. If it bothered him, he didn't show it.

'Bye, Bwin.' Her little girl both broke and raised the tension.

He gave her another sad smile. 'Bye, Harper.'

Then he turned to Mia. 'Could you give me your contact details? For the...' he had the good grace to lower his voice '...test.'

So he hadn't changed his mind. Her stomach was in knots, her heart deflating. In a flat tone, she gave him her details.

'Okay.' He nodded as he put them into his phone. The smile was gone.

Then, in another beat, so was he.

Again.

CHAPTER FOUR

THE LONG NIGHT turned into an even longer six days that Mia thought would never end. She helped clean up the camp, dropped Harper off at nursery, then returned home to find her little cottage under a couple of feet of water. She managed to save what she could, called the insurance company then walked to work to find a very soggy clinic. Sometimes, even the best of buildings couldn't stop a very determined storm.

She'd been cleaning up for six days. It felt like six years.

And every moment was dogged by thoughts of Brin. Flashbacks to that night and the sexy way he'd looked at her intersected with his expression when she'd told him about Harper. All the while her heart jumped and jittered. She was exhausted physically, mentally and emotionally.

Looking forward to clocking off for the weekend, she was putting the closed sign on the clinic door when Carly bounded in. 'Hey, Mia! How's things?'

Mia grinned, always pleased to see her friend. 'You look very energised! Clearly you haven't been elbow-deep in flood water and storm damage for the last few days.'

'We were lucky our cottage stayed reasonably dry. But, anyway, I barely noticed. I am fuelled by love.' Carly waved her hand in the air and giggled. 'And I can't believe I even said that.'

'Oh, God, please—you're making me nauseous.' But it was so lovely to see Carly find happiness again after so many years in the dark, grieving for her beloved Rafferty. Mia felt a tinge of envy.

'I'm making me nauseous.' Carly giggled again. 'Sorry. Do you need a hand?'

'No, I'm done. Ready for the weekend.' Mia walked back to the reception desk and powered down the computer.

Carly leaned against the door jamb. 'Hey, are you okay? I've been worried about you all week. You seem, I don't know, distracted. Upset.'

And for good reason. 'I'm fine, honestly.'

'And yet you don't look it. What's wrong, hun?' Carly walked across the room and frowned sadly over the desk at her. 'Did the storm bring back some bad memories?'

Oh, hell.

Mia didn't need sympathy. She'd never asked anyone for help or discussed her thoughts and feelings, at least not since her mum had died.

God, she missed her. But Carly was her best friend; they'd shared so much grief and trauma together, and she'd kept secrets from her for too long. Plus, she was going to explode if she didn't talk this through with someone.

She looked up at her friend and grimaced. 'Good memories, actually.'

Carly's frown deepened. 'I'm sorry?'

Oops, her mouth was running away. If she started to talk, she didn't know if she would be able to stop. 'Nothing. Ignore me.'

'Mia Edwards, what are you not telling me?' Carly peered at her suspiciously. 'Come on, talk to me. Sometimes it helps to share stuff. What good times are we talking here, you dark horse?'

'Oh, God. I need to tell someone before I go completely mad.' Mia took a deep breath and blew it out slowly. 'You remember Brin…from the other night?'

'The gorgeous Irish paramedic?' Carly shrugged at Mia's frown. 'Can't blame a girl for noticing.'

'Yes. That Brin.'

'I saw you two outside, deep in conversation. What was that all about?' Carly's frown melted into a huge smile. 'Oh, my God. He asked you out?'

'It's a little more complicated than that.'

Carly walked round the desk and leaned against it, peering closely at Mia. 'Oh?'

Mia took another deep breath. 'Well…he's…he's Harper's father.'

Her friend's eyes almost popped out of her head. She opened her mouth, closed it and opened it again. 'What? I think I might need my ears syringed—I thought you said he's Harper's dad.'

'I did. He is.' Mia watched her friend's reaction, which appeared to go from shock to confusion to delight to worry. Kind of how Mia felt but nowhere near as intense.

Carly grimaced too. 'I think I'm going to have to sit down. Every time I've tried to bring up the subject, you've hedged or flat out refused to say anything. But Brin? He's… Wow… I don't believe it.'

You're not the only one.

Mia stood and started to pace across the floor. 'I didn't think telling you about him was relevant. It was a one-night thing, fun and exciting, never to be repeated.'

'I guessed that much already. When you came back from that party you were different, somehow. Can't quite explain it. But you had a definite smile on your face. You had a great time.'

'We did. It was meant to be just a bit of fun. I didn't even tell him my real name. We didn't talk jobs. It wasn't an interview. It was sex. Great sex.'

Carly's eyes widened. 'Good. Okay. Why not? No judgement here.'

'Then he went off travelling. There were a

lot of things I didn't know about him…like his surname, for a start. When I found out I was pregnant, I couldn't just call him and tell him. I couldn't find him.'

'And now he's come back.' Her eyes narrowed. 'For you?'

Mia shook her head, ignoring the sting in her chest. 'No. He got a job here. He's just doing Lewis a favour, I think. Plus, it's a promotion. But he was in Perth—Perth in Australia, not Perth in Scotland. Oh, and I'm babbling. I'm just… thrown.'

Carly patted the chair next to her. 'This is so unlike you, Mia. Come and sit down. You never panic. Does he know about Harper?'

Mia preferred to pace. 'Yes. I told him as soon as I could. It seemed only fair.'

'And?' Carly bugged her eyes. 'And?'

'He demanded a DNA test. I received a call from a company in Auckland the morning after the storm, confirming my details, so he must have contacted them the minute he left here. They couriered over a test pack, I did Harper's mouth swab and sent it back the same day. The results will be emailed in the next few days.'

Carly exhaled on a smile. 'That's good news, right?'

Mia stopped pacing. 'Why?'

'It means he's considering things. He wants a quick answer.'

Mia hadn't considered that. 'Why won't he just believe me?'

'Why should he?'

Mia stared at her friend. Wasn't it obvious? 'Because I wouldn't lie about something like this. I mean, I know it's a shock, but it's very clear he doesn't trust me. In fact, he wasn't very nice about the whole thing. Nothing like the kind guy I remember. Showing his true colours, eh?'

Carly scowled. 'To be honest, Mia, you only had one night with him. That's not long enough to get to know or trust someone. He might think you want to sue him for back-dated child support, or God knows what. He's right to be wary.'

Oh, Carly had all the reasonable answers. 'I wouldn't do anything like that. And we clicked, Carly. The chemistry was real, off the scale. But maybe I was wrong about him. Maybe he's the kind of man who's going to run. Maybe Brin O'Connor is just a heartless, unreliable jerk I don't want my daughter to get involved with.'

Never mind about me.

A shiver in the atmosphere had her turning to look towards the door. Carly had left it open and a figure had walked in. He was tall, dark-haired and gorgeous, looking every bit as shocked at her words as he had been when she'd stepped on to the helicopter.

Despite everything, Mia's heart did a little dance at the sight of him, while her head told it to quieten the hell down. This man could be dangerous to her equilibrium and her heart, not to mention to her daughter's.

Brin was back.

Great.

He'd heard her not-so-glowing description of him. And she knew he'd heard. *Awkward.*

Both women were staring at him, mouths open. For a split second he felt like doing exactly what she thought he'd do—running. Not from Harper and her, but from the feelings swirling in his chest. From the panic and immediate desire at seeing her again. From the dismay that she didn't seem to like him much. That he was going to be just like his brother: a royal jerk.

Ex-brother. *Persona non grata.*

But the last ferry had pulled out of the harbour and he was stuck here, at least for the night. And, no matter how far he ran, he couldn't escape himself, could he?

Why the hell he'd come back, he wasn't sure. But, the minute he'd clocked off for two days, he'd rushed home, packed a bag and ran for the ferry. He hadn't been able to fight the need to be here.

He didn't know what he was expecting or looking for. But here he was. 'Hey, Mia. Hi, Carly.'

The two women glanced at each other. Carly gave Mia a hug and, loudly enough for him to hear and heed the hidden warning, she whispered in her Kiwi-English accent, 'Love you, Mia. Call me if you need me. I'll come straight over.'

Then she nodded at him and left.

He wanted to smile. It was good to know Mia had people who had her back. Who'd hopefully been there for her over the last few years, given she had no family now, except Harper.

His family…

He wasn't very nice. He was unreliable.

The words pierced his chest. He'd spent all thirty-four years of his life trying to be kind, fair and honest, the exact opposite of his father and brother. He'd been there for Niamh at every step, all the firsts.

'Hey, Mia.'

'Brin.' Her eyes were dark, her posture rigid, far from the carefree woman he remembered. But hell, she was so beautiful, just looking at her made his chest heat.

He inhaled. 'Look, I wanted to apologise for the way I behaved the other day…night. You know…' God, he was making a mess of this.

Her hands were on her hips. 'You could have just called or emailed. Actually, yes, an email would have been better. It would have saved you a trip.'

'I…wanted to see you face-to-face. Things are always better that way. I was shocked and I acted badly. I can be nice. I *am* nice.' Was the real truth that he'd wanted to see her face? He hadn't stopped thinking about her all week. Not just because of Harper, although she'd been in his head all week too, and what the future might hold. *If* she was his daughter.

But Mia had been at the forefront of his mind too much: the soft sway of her hips; the curve of her lips; her scent that he recognised even now, all these years later. It was something floral and intoxicating—a little musk.

He tried for a smile, which was not reflected by her face as she said, 'Has the test result come back? Only, it hadn't last time I checked my emails.'

'What? No. Not the last time I checked either.' He'd been refreshing his email account endlessly for the last few hours. His nerves were shredded, and hers too, judging by her curt attitude. Although, that could also likely be because of the way he'd responded to her news the other day.

Her eyebrows rose. 'So, you're here because…?'

'I thought we needed to talk some more.'

'No. Not until the DNA results come through.'

Wow, this was a turnaround. This was not a woman who wanted someone to fund her child's education and expenses. Not that he'd thought that about Mia, but it happened. It had happened to him.

She held up a palm and continued. 'In fact, I

don't want you getting involved with my daughter until I know I can trust you, Brin O'Connor.'

He was not his father. He would not walk away from his responsibilities. He was not his brother. He would not betray his family.

But she knew nothing about him, really. They'd only shared one night, after all. 'Fair enough. I wouldn't trust me either. Maybe I am just a heartless…what was it?…jerk?'

Red bloomed in her cheeks. 'I—'

'Hey there!' Owen popped his head round the door. 'There you go, Harper. Here's your mummy. Oh hey, Brin, good to see you.'

The little girl ran into the room, beaming. 'Mumma! Mumma!'

And your daddy?

Brin tried to dampen down the flicker of hope in his chest. He didn't want to be this little girl's father. He didn't want to get involved with this family, not if it meant putting his heart at risk.

He didn't know the DNA results yet but still his whole body smiled at the toddler running across the room, her arms outstretched as she reached her mum.

'Hi there, sweetie. Did you have a good day at nursery?' Mia bent, picked Harper up, kissed her and whirled her round, all rigidity and stuffiness gone. Harper put her chubby hands on her mum's face and gave her a kiss. Mia's eyes were brown and her hair blonde, in stark contrast to her daughter's blue eyes and black curls. But the smile…that was pure Mia.

Something tightened in his chest and he realised, with a shock, that it was a kind of yearning…for these two? For that feeling of warmth at the end of a hard week? For someone to greet him with a smile? For *his people*?

Hell, one minute in their company and he was jelly. He didn't have any people. He knew that well enough. And he was just fine on his own.

Why had he come here?

What a mistake to think he might fix some of this mess he'd found himself in. He should get on the first ferry out tomorrow morning.

Owen was looking at him. 'What's happened? Is there an evac?' He looked at Mia. 'Why didn't you call me?'

She held her hand up and gave the doctor a wavering smile.

'No.'

'No.'

They spoke at the same time, and he heard the panic in her voice mirror the same feelings in his chest. 'Stand down, doc. There's no emergency. I'm just here for the weekend; thought I'd check the place out.'

'Well, you wouldn't believe a storm blew through last week, eh?' Owen glanced out at the dazzling sunshine outside. 'It's a stunning day and good forecast.'

A little cold in here, though.

'Weekend?' Mia blinked.

But before any of them could say anything more, Harper ran across to Brin and offered him her blanket. His heart folded. Oh God, this was their game now. She looked so eager to play, he couldn't resist.

He bent down and threw the blanket over Harper's face, waiting for the giggle. It quickly came and felt like sunshine in his chest.

Sunshine that scudded under a cloud as Mia asked flatly, 'Where are you staying?'

'B and B down the road. Next to the yacht club.'

Totally oblivious to the dynamic between Brin and Mia, Owen nodded. 'Ah, Wiremu's place. He'll look after you. But you should have called me. You are more than welcome to stay at ours for free. Any time.' His young boy was tugging at his hand. 'Daddy! Come on. Kayaking with Carly.'

'Duty calls.' Owen rolled his eyes and laughed. 'Hey, mate, what do you have planned while you're here?'

'Not much, really. A hike, maybe a kayak. Relaxing.' As if that was going to be possible, being so close to Mia. 'Not sure.'

'I don't suppose you could help out at the regatta tomorrow? It's just me and Mia and we could do with another pair of hands, especially as we'll have our kids with us.'

'Regatta?' Brin looked from Owen to Mia then back again. Mia's stony expression had returned and her eyes were blazing, as if she was trying to send him some sort of message. Probably along the lines of, *don't say yes*.

Owen nodded and pointed to a poster on the wall. 'Boat race. Leaving the yacht club at nine o'clock, but the festivities will go on all morning. There's a sausage sizzle and craft fair. We're running the medical tent—giving out sunscreen, raising awareness of being sun- and sea-smart. Plus, any injuries. It's usually just the odd splinter. Nothing you can't handle.'

He felt the weight of Mia's stare on his back, but he could hardly say no, could he? He didn't have any other plans, the island was small and he could probably explore it all in one afternoon. He had until Sunday evening here. 'It'll give me something to do. Sure.'

Owen nodded as he made his way to the door. 'Great. Cheers, mate. See you in the morning, then.'

Then there was just the three of them—Mia, Harper and him.

There wasn't any point staying around for more of this awkward exchange, so he followed in Owen's wake towards the door, his chest aching a little. God knew what he'd expected but it wasn't to feel so deflated. But yeah…he'd been delusional to think Mia would be as excited about his visit as he was.

He turned for a last look. 'I'll see you tomorrow.'

'Brin. Wait.' She looked as if she was having a struggle between her head and her heart. More like between being polite and unfriendly.

His chest warmed in anticipation. 'Yes?'

'Look, there aren't many places to eat on the island, and I don't imagine you've brought much food with you.'

'I was going to eat at the yacht club—apparently they do excellent food.'

'They do. And we always have a table there on a Friday, eh, Harper? Go to see Wiremu for some hot chips?'

As Harper did a happy wiggle and repeated, 'Hot chips, hot chips…' on a loop, Mia's expression became guarded.

'It's just a treat. We eat healthily the rest of the time. She has a very balanced diet for her growing needs.'

He laughed. 'You don't want to know what rubbish I eat most of the time. Whatever I can stuff in my mouth between call-outs, and ramen if I'm being fancy. I am not judging. A portion of hot chips is perfect for a day like today.'

The guardedness slipped a little into a sort-of smile. 'Which is what, exactly?'

Oh, so many things. Joy at little Harper's happy squeals when she'd played their game. Pride at the burgeoning friendship with Owen. All of it mixed with trepidation, panic and confusion about potentially being a father, and the question of Mia… whose smile, when it came, entranced him, reeled him in, speared his chest.

He settled on, 'Difficult?'

Her shoulders finally dropped, and she blew out a long sigh. 'Yes. Difficult indeed.'

'I probably should have prepared you for me turning up again out of the blue. I'm sorry. Next time I will most definitely call.'

Her eyes widened. 'Next time?'

'Yes. Next time.' If he was this girl's father, there would be many, many times. He just had to try and wrestle his attraction to Mia under control. Because he couldn't let anything derail his relationship with Harper. Nothing could happen between Mia and him—nothing at all. 'I don't want it to be difficult.'

'Me neither.'

He blew out a breath and couldn't help smiling. Maybe they'd reached a detente? 'So how about we have a chat? Nothing heavy. Just an end-of-the-week catch-up over hot chips.'

'Okay, yes. Sounds good.' She nodded and smiled a really wide grin. Boy, that blew his mind and had his skin, his whole body, prickling with heat.

Which was a warning sign he needed to listen to.

CHAPTER FIVE

Of course, everyone remembered Brin from the storm, and they were all pleased to see him, and not even a little taken aback that he was with Mia and Harper.

It seemed as if Mia was the only one taken aback by his sudden appearance. Harper was thrilled. Owen seemed happy to have found a new buddy, offering him a free place to stay and asking him to help out.

After placing their order, they sat outside at her usual table, overlooking the small marina. Brin's eyebrows rose as he scanned the myriad yachts, launches and dinghies in the bay. 'Wow, there are a lot of boats here.'

'It's not usually like this. They're here for the regatta.'

'It's got a great vibe.' He tapped his foot along to a four-piece band playing summer classics and she relaxed a little. Sure, her heart had stalled when he'd walked into the clinic, but now… Now she needed—wanted—to try and smooth things out for Harper's sake.

She was glad to be in the warmth of the late-afternoon sun, able to breathe a bit more freely, rather than being confined in a small room with him. He dominated every space and assaulted her senses with his intoxicating scent and gorgeous eyes.

Right now, he was sitting next to Harper and playing 'hide the teddy'. The way he looked at their child snagged her heart. He was the father: there was no doubt, never any doubt at all. But seeing the way they were together proved it beyond anything.

It was hard to think rationally around him but they had important things to discuss. She wasn't going to let him barrel over her parenting with his ideas or change the routine she'd developed with her little girl.

Might he take her away? Oh, God, no. He couldn't do that. Could he?

'Hey.' He dipped his head to look at her across the table, catching her gaze and giving her a smile. 'You zoned out for a minute. I was just saying, this is an idyllic place to grow up. Did you grow up here too? Or somewhere else?'

'Sorry, I was miles away.' She'd been too engrossed in panicked fantasies to be in the present. 'Here. At the camp, actually. My parents used to run the place.'

'Wow. I bet you ran wild with all that bush out the back.'

'Not at all. I wasn't allowed to go too far from the cottage, not until I got older. And I learnt to share all my things from a young age, my home and my very large garden, not just with my brother but with kids from all over the *motu* who had come to learn sailing and bush skills.'

'Motu?' He shook his head.

'It means "country". Sorry.'

'Don't be. I'm getting used to the way Kiwis slip *te reo Māori* into their sentences. It's cool. I wish I'd learnt Gaelic at school.'

'Do you miss Ireland?'

'It's a pretty place. A lot of weather. A bit like here.'

She frowned. 'That's not an answer. Do you have family there?'

Did Harper have family there? Cousins, aunties and uncles he might want her to meet?

His jaw tightened. 'Not any more.'

'No one?' He was like her, then, all alone in the world. She should have been relieved but there was something in the way he looked at her, as if he was trying to decide what to say, before he settled on, 'No one.'

She wasn't sure he was being completely honest here. But she imagined he had his reasons and decided not to push him—yet. 'That's too sad. I mean, growing up here wasn't all roses. My brother could be a royal pain sometimes. Boy, could we fight.'

Brin's jaw relaxed. 'Nothing like having a sibling to keep you grounded, right?'

They both looked at Harper and Mia's stomach felt like a stone. A sibling? Another baby?

He winced. 'I'm sorry, that was careless of me. You must miss your brother very much.'

'I do.' Not wanting to dwell on her own tragedy she asked, 'Your parents…?'

'Mum died a few years ago.' He shrugged but she could see the pain in his eyes.

'I'm sorry. And your dad…?' She let her words fade, hoping he hadn't had the same kind of tragedy she'd had.

'Left. Mammy said he was good at making babies but terrible at caring for them.' His blue eyes darkened. 'I have different things to say about him.'

'Like what?' Babies…plural. What had happened to his siblings?

He cautiously flicked his eyes towards Harper. 'I'm not going to ruin this evening. The best thing said about my da is nothing at all.' His tone was light again but there were dark edges to his eyes. There was more to this story but he clearly wasn't going to talk about it here or now.

Harper tugged at her sleeve. 'Mumma. Icecream, please?'

'Finish your dinner first, then we'll decide.'

She looked up to see Brin watching the interaction and her mood took a nosedive. 'You probably think I'm too soft on her.'

'I'm not going to judge how you've brought her up.' He winked at Harper, who instinctively knew they were talking about her, so gave them both a beaming smile. He chuckled. 'Butter wouldn't melt, eh? She's an angel. Great manners. Bright as a button. She's happy, that's the most important thing.'

He sounded almost as proud of their daughter as she felt. 'I'm glad you think so.'

He dipped a chip into some aioli then slipped it into his mouth. 'You were right, Mia. These are some great chips.'

'Tomorrow you should try the steak-and-cheese pies—award-winning. It's blue cheese too. The best.'

'Stop it, temptress.' He bugged his eyes at her but there was something more there: the glitter and tease she'd been so attracted to *before*.

Fantasies of a very different kind slipped into her head. Of her holding him, kissing him…and more. And, oh yes, she wanted to tempt him, to allow herself to fall into flirting with him, just like before.

But she couldn't. She wiped Harper's hands with a tissue. 'Right, missy. Time to get going.'

'Ice-cream?' her daughter asked hopefully but she looked exhausted.

Mia knew her daughter well enough to see that a tantrum was on the horizon. 'We'll have some at home. We've got hokey-pokey, your favourite.'

Brin was still looking at Mia, the light very much in his eyes as he watched her. 'Thanks for this, Mia.'

'It's no trouble.'

He walked with them down the steps and onto the path that ran between the buildings and the marina. 'I should make sure you get home safely.'

'You just did.' She laughed.

He frowned then followed her pointed finger to the house three doors down from where they were standing: her old villa, painted white wood with a row of sandbags along the ground at the front. It was small, cosy and needed a new coat of paint. But it had potential and an amazing view of the marina and across the bay. Mia loved it.

His eyebrows rose. 'Cute house. The sandbags are from the storm?'

'Yes.' She sighed. 'The house needed work before the storm, but it's worse now. The carpet in the front room got saturated and I had to lift everything I could to waist height. Some of Harper's toys started to float away but we rescued them.'

'Sounds bad.'

'Not as bad as some. In the end, the water didn't get as high as the electricity sockets, or we'd really be in a pickle.'

'You should have told me.'

'And you'd have done what? You were too busy choppering people to hospital.'

He grimaced. 'Given you support, at least.'

'It's okay. We weren't exactly talking, were we?'

A shadow slid across his face. 'I think we both needed a bit of space.'

'I know I did.' She was glad he understood her reluctance to dive right in. Glad, too, that he was serious about doing the right thing. 'We're okay and that's the main thing. I've spent the last few days drying everything out and getting air into the rooms. Coupled with that, everywhere needs a decent coat of paint. And I need a new kitchen, which I've ordered and am beyond excited about, which is a thing I never thought I'd say, or be. Excited about a kitchen? Where is that Mia who wanted to travel and get a tattoo and play the drums?'

'She's still there.' His grin was infectious. 'Drums? Wicked.'

She laughed. 'No. Terrible, actually.'

'Well, I see her—playing terrible drums and getting a tattoo.'

'And getting all hot over paint shades.' She was probably babbling and talking nonsense.

I see her.

His words almost whipped her breath away and made her head whirl a little. Did he see the real Mia, the way he had that night? Mia stripped bare and raw… Her body prickled at the memory. No…it was at having him here, so close. It was that smile; his touch. *God*, he'd felt so good. He'd kissed like a demon too.

Her insides started to melt. She was getting hot over a lot more than paint shades. 'You don't want to hear about all this.'

'I do, actually.' Probably because he wanted to make sure Harper was living in a sanitary, habitable house. 'I could… No.'

He shook his head and took a step back.

Her heart hammered. What had he been about to say? 'You could…?'

Come in?

Help renovate?

Kiss me?

That last thought slid to the front of her mind, obliterating all reasoning. To kiss him, taste him, hold him close… So tantalisingly tempting and so *not* a good idea.

'Mumma.' Harper put out her hands to be picked up and Mia hauled her onto her hip. Immediately, Harper laid her head on Mia's shoulder, stuck her thumb in her mouth and rubbed the satin edge of her blanket between her fingers.

Brin's eyes softened as he looked at his daughter. 'Looks like it's someone's bedtime.'

'Yes, I think we've had enough excitement for one day.' Mia looked up at him. Had she imagined the flicker of awareness in his eyes? The subtle slide of his gaze from her eyes to her mouth? The flare of…something?

Deep in her belly, she felt a responsive stirring of desire. Heat hit her cheeks and she started to turn away before he saw it.

'Mia Edwards.' Her name sounded like poetry, with the way he'd said it, and she wanted him to say it over and over. She was bewitched by the gentle lilt of his accent. Again.

She turned back to get a glimpse of him. Again. 'Yes, Brin O'Connor?' The way she replied sounded wanton.

'Sleep well.' The smile he gave her was filled with generosity, with a good helping of seductiveness.

She wasn't sure she was going to sleep at all, with images of him running through her mind. 'Good night, Brin. See you in the morning.'

'Definitely.' He scuffed his fingertips through Harper's hair. 'Night-night, little one.'

The effect of his smile, his warmth and…everything…had her wishing things had been different. Had her wanting him to touch her.

She wanted his hands on her. Wanted his mouth on her…everywhere.

No. That couldn't happen. She'd lost everything she'd loved when her family had been drowned. Then she'd found solace and more than enough love in her daughter. It had been a hard road, getting to this state of tranquillity. She liked being calm, and prided herself on being efficient, friendly and kind, and a respected member of the island community. She didn't want or need a man to upset everything she'd worked so hard for.

She wasn't going to risk losing another love again or change her hard-won, happy life here. She had her sanity, her equilibrium. Her emotions had been wrangled under control. She did not want to be out of control. She was going to be resolutely single. For the rest of her life.

She nodded at him. 'See you.' And then she went into her house, hoping its cool interior would soothe the heat in her body.

Thirty minutes later she was putting a bathed and very sleepy Harper to bed when her phone pinged.

It was an incoming email from the DNA test lab.

Her heart rattled but she couldn't understand why. She knew the facts. But the thought of having Brin in her life made her anxious, excited and panicked. The attraction to him was growing stronger and she didn't know how to deal with it.

He could break her heart. Worse, he could break her daughter's by moving on.

She slid her phone into her jeans pocket, kissed her…*their*…now-sleeping daughter on the cheek and left the room.

Truth was on her side. But knowing that didn't settle the panic. Things were going to change, regardless of whether she wanted them to or not.

After clearing up the mess from this morning's rush to get out of the house to nursery and work, she needed some peace and fresh air, so opened the front door and set up her deck chair on the kerb side. The sky was cloudless with a thick slick of purple stars and the Milky Way.

Up the road at the yacht club, people were laughing. The lap of water against the jetty that usually lulled her did nothing to soothe her nerves.

Brin O'Connor was going to be in her daughter's life and, inevitably, in Mia's too. She needed to learn how to deal with it.

And not think about kissing him again.

CHAPTER SIX

So HE WAS a father. A real one this time. Although he'd feel as if Niamh was his daughter for the rest of his life, someone else was her daddy now.

Brin shoved his phone back into his pocket and tried to breathe. The bedroom was stuffy. He opened a window and stood at it, trying to shift the ache in his lungs. It wasn't working. He needed to be outside and feel the fresh night air against his skin.

He ran downstairs and out the front door into the cool evening, stuck his hands into his jeans pockets and headed along the road, trying to work out how to navigate this strange situation. Last time it had been easy, as he'd lived with Niamh's mother. But this time? He had no idea. And he'd already missed so much. He was suddenly greedy to know everything about Harper.

Sure, he already knew the basics. His daughter had pilfered a piece of his heart that he knew he'd never get back. Her smile was like sunshine. Her tears pierced his chest. He'd do everything in his power to protect her and love her. Anything else was icing on the cake.

And Mia? His pulse quickened at the thought of her. The glitter in her eyes when he'd jokingly called her a temptress…over a pie! The effect on him had been instant, a direct arrow to his groin. But also…and far more dangerously…to his heart.

Ah, Mia.

The pull to her was getting hard to ignore.

As if the Fates were looking down and playing games, she appeared outside her house, carrying a mug of steaming liquid. Her eyes widened as he approached.

He couldn't exactly turn round and walk away. 'Mia?'

She nodded and put her mug on the window-sill 'You got the email?'

An email that had changed his life. 'She's my daughter.'

'Yes. I told you. You are the only person I've had sex with in…well, you know.' Her cheeks reddened. 'A very long time.'

He didn't want to think of her having sex with anyone but him—ever. 'So, what do we do now?'

She rubbed her palms down her thighs. She'd changed out of her nurse's scrubs into a T-shirt that skimmed her curves, and shorts that high-lighted her gorgeous legs. 'I have no idea.'

'Do you want me to be involved?'

'Oh, Brin, yes of course. You're her father, you have every right.' She exhaled. 'But…can I be honest with you?'

'Always. Please. I want to know what you're thinking.'

She worried at her bottom lip. 'She's been just mine for so long. I've never had to think about sharing her and now I'm worried.'

'You think I might…what?'

'I don't know. Take her away?' She looked haunted at the thought, bereft. 'To Ireland.'

Never. 'God, Mia. No way. This is her home.' He'd lived the nightmare of having his child cruelly taken away from him, and he wasn't about to inflict that poison on someone else.

Unless, of course, it was his brother. Who, while not being in a relationship with Niamh's mother, was still seeing Niamh on a regular basis.

Mo stór.

Mia pierced him with a dark look. She still didn't trust him. 'And where is your home?'

Good question.

'I haven't had one for a long time.'

'But it's not here, right? You've already left here once, looking for more excitement.' She raised her palm. 'It's not Australia. It's not Ireland. You're still looking. It could be somewhere far away. You're a city boy, right? Dublin and Perth, not a tiny community on an island in the middle of nowhere.'

'Whoa. I've known about her for less than a week. I've got no plans to take her anywhere. I'd like to get to know her. To spend time with her.' He leaned against the wall and looked at her. She was so defensive, protective...*good*. Their daughter needed a strong woman like Mia in her life. But she'd done it all on her own and he couldn't imagine how she'd managed. 'Tell me about it.'

She frowned. 'About what?'

'All of it. The birth. Her firsts.'

Her eyebrows rose. 'Oh, sure... Well, I've got child-bearing hips, so the pregnancy was fine.' She ran her hands over her hips, drawing his eyes down.

She had an amazing body with which she'd carried and given birth to his child. He could barely breathe at the thought, and at what he'd missed. 'No complications?'

'None.' She smiled. 'Quick and easy.'

'Where?'

'Here. At the camp.' Her gaze flitted across the bay. 'A home birth.'

'Wasn't that a bit risky?'

'Actually, a surprise. I wasn't due for another couple of weeks and I'd planned to go over to the city in good time. But Harper was in a hurry.' Her eyes had a faraway look about them. She smiled and rubbed her belly and he ached to press his fingers there. He wondered what it would have been like to feel the swell of his child inside her.

'Luckily Anahera's well used to helping deliver babies in extremis. And, double luck, I had a midwife friend staying on the island. And Carly, of course. My three musketeers. Everything was fine. Once we'd delivered her and I felt well enough, we went over to the mainland to get checked out with the doctor.'

'Wasn't Owen here?'

'No, he's new. We didn't have a doctor then.'

'Who helped you afterwards? Cooked meals, made sure you got some rest?'

'Mother hen.' She nudged him and laughed. 'I moved into Carly's cottage for the first few weeks after Harper was born and she looked after me. She's really good family.'

This was confusing. He was sure Carly was from England. 'She's your family? But she has an English accent. You're very Kiwi.'

Mia smiled. 'Oh, of course, I keep forgetting you don't know the history. She was married to my brother. We're not blood family. Sisters by marriage, best friends by choice.'

A far cry from his relationship with his brother. Blood wasn't always thicker. 'Sometimes that's better than the real thing.'

'Oh?' Her eyebrows rose in question and he realised she was too easy to talk to.

'Nah. No. Not going there.'

Her eyebrows slumped into a frown and he could see her emotionally retreat at his refusal to answer her question. But he wasn't going to taint this conversation with tales of his broken family. There was too much he was greedy to know about Harper, about them both. 'Tell me about my girl.'

Mia's eyes grew soft and he wasn't sure if he saw a sheen of tears there. But she looked away and cleared her throat. 'She was a big baby. Three-point-eight kilogrammes, and long. She's got your long legs, Brin.'

Her gaze drifted down his body then back to capture his gaze. He saw pride and love there as she talked about Harper. She looked so beautiful, it made his heart hurt. He remembered the way she'd been so soft in his arms. The feel of her skin against his. The way she'd tasted.

'She's got your smile.' He wasn't sure what else to do or say. He knew what he *wanted* to do. But he was not going to kiss Mia Edwards.

'She's a good kid. My heart.' She put her hand on her chest. 'Please don't upset her.'

'Of course not. At least, I'll try not to. But you know how teenagers can be sometimes. I'm bound to be embarrassing at some point.'

'Teenagers?' She chuckled. 'She's barely turned two.'

'They start early these days. Grow up too fast.' But she turned serious. 'I meant, please don't say you're going to do something and then not do it. Turn up on time. Be reliable.'

'Hey.' He touched her shoulder. 'I'm not a bad guy.'

'I know. I couldn't bear it if you hurt her.'

That thought pierced him too. 'I won't. At least, I'll try not to.'

She nodded. 'Good. And it's going to be confusing for her if you suddenly start being around all the time.'

'I know. Slowly does it. Will she understand if we tell her?'

'I…don't know. Let's see how it pans out.'

He wanted Harper to know who he was right now but needed to take Mia's lead on this. 'Okay. And I will want regular visits. I need to get to know her after everything I've missed.' In case she took that as a criticism, he added, 'It must have been hard, facing a future as a solo mum with no grandparents to help out.'

'Yes. But everyone here's family.'

'I get that feeling. It's a good place.'

'I was well looked after. We both were. Harper is Rāwhiti Island's baby.'

'So, I'd better be careful?' He laughed, but knew it was the truth. Also, that leaving here and living somewhere else was not on Mia's radar. This was her home.

Where was his? Currently Auckland, where his job was. It wasn't a thousand miles away but it was hardly next door. And she was right: he'd never planned it to be permanent.

'Don't say you haven't been warned.' She chuckled, picked up her mug and frowned. 'My tea's gone cold. You want one?'

'Are you sure?'

'I think we can manage to be civil, right?'

'More than civil.' He followed her into her house. Maybe she was starting to trust him after all.

The front door led straight into a lounge in disarray. A blue sofa and two cosy-looking blue-and-white-checked chairs had been pushed against the back wall. Piled on top of them were a box of toys and a basket of laundry. There was no carpet, just bare floorboards. A dehumidifier hummed in the corner. It was in disarray, but the overriding scent was lavender cleaning fluid, and it was spotlessly clean.

She watched him take it all in. 'I've had the insurance people over and there's a new carpet coming. Everything else is salvageable. It's safe. She's not living in squalor.'

'Jeez, Mia, I don't think that. You're amazing to have done all this on your own.' He wanted to scoop them up, take them back to his apartment on the mainland and look after them. But he got the impression Mia wouldn't let that happen in a million years.

'I made it into a game for Harper. She was a good little helper.'

'If you need anything, let me know.'

She shook her head. 'I've got this. I can manage just fine.'

On my own. Like the last three years.

The unspoken words filled the room.

'Mia, I mean it. Let me help.' But he knew she was a resilient, independent woman. She would ask for help *if* she needed it, not because he thought she did. 'I know you've probably been saying "I've got this" for the last three years, but you don't have to do this on your own any more.'

She pressed her lips together and took a deep breath. 'Guess I'm not very good at sharing after all.'

'Baby steps, right?'

She looked grateful he hadn't pushed the issue. 'Yep. Baby steps.'

Despite the flooding there were still photographs of his daughter on every wall: as a tiny new-born, strapped to Carly in a sling; at her first birthday, with a paper hat on; in the garden. And so many with her mum, giddy with pride. He rubbed his fist against the ache in his chest as he stopped at one where Harper was in a pink party dress and Mia was bent over, holding her hands. They looked as if they were dancing at a party. He traced the outline of his daughter's face. 'She's beautiful.'

Mia came and stood next to him, close enough to touch. And, man, he wanted to. She sighed. 'My little ray of sunshine. That was at Anahera's youngest's wedding in the yacht club.'

He laughed. 'You weren't escaping *Dancing Queen* that time?'

'You remembered.' She looked up at him, her brown eyes alight, her mouth a crescent of joy. 'Your daughter loves to dance, Brin. *Dancing Queen* is her favourite song. After *Baby Shark*, of course.'

'She's got great taste.'

She frowned. 'Have you ever heard *Baby Shark*?'

'No, thank you.'

She looked at the photograph. 'I'm sorry you missed those years. We should have stayed in touch.' She moved slightly and her hand brushed against his. The air seemed to sizzle around them. He struggled to fill his lungs with the Mia-scented air.

'I wish we had.'

She turned to face him, so close her fingers pressed against his. Her smile was soft and sexy, her eyes searching his. And suddenly it was three years ago. Just him, her and the most amazing night ahead.

He reached for her hand, entwining his fingers with hers. She looked down at them, a little gasp escaping her lips. But she didn't pull away;

instead, she looked back at him. A wary smile played on her lips, as if she was as confused by all of this as he was.

A beat passed, two…the atmosphere thickened with need. He wanted to…everything. He wanted her so damned much. Which was crazy and messed up because he knew that anything between them would be a risk to him, to him seeing his daughter and to his equilibrium. But she held his gaze and he couldn't, wouldn't, look away.

It was all too much too soon. It was crazy to feel like this. He ran his thumb over hers. 'God, Mia…'

'Yes?' Her breath stuttered in her chest, her mouth a fraction open.

He saw it then, in her eyes: a mirrored need. The chemistry was real and raw. It was like the first time, an incomprehensible attraction. She was the only thing he was aware of: her sensual mouth; her soft skin; her sultry eyes. Just… Mia.

Not wanting to let go of her, he slid the fingers of his free hand across her cheek, cupping her face. Her mouth was inches away. He could feel her hitched breath against his jaw. Maybe she didn't trust him, maybe she did. But she wanted this.

He should have walked away then, knowing that they were on a trajectory that could only end in disaster. But she grasped his wrist, held it in place then rose up on tiptoes and pressed her mouth against his.

'God. Mia.'

He let go of her hand and slid his fingers across her other cheek to her hairline. His heart raced. His chest constricted. His skin felt too tight.

His head screamed at him to go. But he couldn't.

She tasted exactly as he remembered: intoxicating and fresh, and of the herbal tea she'd sipped. Of something pure Mia. Her body fitted against his and he felt the press of her breasts against his chest. It felt like an extension of that night, without three years in between. No re-learning, just pleasure and need.

A squeak of a cry came from another room.

Harper. His daughter. She was the most important person in all of this. He couldn't think this was going to end in happy families. It never did. In fact, he wasn't sure that such a thing existed.

He pulled away, his body shaking. 'Look, sorry. That shouldn't have happened. It'll only complicate things.'

Mia nodded quickly, looking turned on and yet torn as she straightened her clothes. 'Brin…yes. Sorry. I need to go to her.'

He watched her disappear into the back recess of the house. He already missed the feel of her in his arms—the soft lips, the hot kisses.

Mia. His heart rattled against his rib cage. Mia and Harper. This was how it could have been:

both parents together, taking it in turns to soothe the little one. The other making tea or pouring wine. An evening shared. A bed shared.

But he'd done all that before and it had broken his goddamned heart.

So, he took a deep breath and reined in all his strength to put one foot in front of the other and walk away.

CHAPTER SEVEN

MIA WAS GLAD of the steady stream of customers at the little gazebo they'd erected outside the clinic, taking her mind off the fact Brin was standing so close to her. And she pushed back the memories of that kiss.

The island was alive with tourists and locals out to watch the boat race. Crowds filled the jetty and thronged the road and beach. There was a happy vibe, which she would normally sink into, but today she felt weird—short-changed, actually. The kiss had been amazing, but nowhere near long enough. Even though they shouldn't have done it in the first place, because it could only muddy things.

How could she be so attracted to this man? She'd never forgotten him, that much was true. She'd dreamt about him. Ached for him. But to have such an immediate and undeniable connection again scared her. There were so many reasons why they needed to keep this purely platonic.

What didn't help was the way Harper gravitated to him all morning, wanting him to play, showing him her shell collection, asking him to fasten her sandals. Watching him with their daughter—the gentle tone of his voice, the patience at the never-ending game of hide-and-seek—had her heart contracting.

The kiss had been such a shock, and so wanted in that moment, she'd been blinded by her need for his touch. But now, in the fresh light of day, and after having ruminated about it for most of the night, she knew that anything between them had to be purely and totally about what was good for Harper.

Kissing Brin was not good for Harper.

Mooning over Brin was not good for Harper.

Thinking about happy families, trying to create something like that, was *not* good. Mia had had one of those once and losing it had made her almost insane with grief. Harper had been a wonderful surprise, but reconciling having a child with her fear of losing her had been difficult. She'd carved out a protected space in her heart for her daughter and now that was all she had the capacity for.

She was not prepared to love anyone else. Because what if she lost them too? She wouldn't be able to cope a second time. So keeping a level head around him would definitely be good.

Owen came out of the clinic, carrying a tray. 'Lemonade for the workers. Is it okay if I finish up now?'

'Sure. There's only an hour until we close up anyway. And we're not exactly run off our feet.' Mia took a glass from the tray as Brin sauntered over after treating someone for a wasp sting. Keeping busy kept him at arm's length.

Owen put the tray on the fold-up table under the gazebo. 'Thanks. I'm meeting Carly and we're taking Mason for a quick swim over in our bay. Would you like us to take Harper too?'

No doubt Carly had already told Owen about the Mia-Harper-Brin saga and, even though he hadn't mentioned anything so far, was the doctor doing a bit of match-making here, or giving them space to talk in private? Did he genuinely want to take Harper to play with his son?

And why was she suddenly suspicious of her friends?

But she looked over at her daughter, who was putting sticking plasters on her doll's knee, and started to feel a bit wobbly about being left here on her own with Brin. There was safety in numbers… 'Oh, she's fine.'

But Harper tugged at Mia's sleeve. '*Please*, Mumma. Swim.'

'It's mighty hot, that's for sure.' Brin smiled at Harper, and Mia read that as a capitulation.

Rather than argue in front of everyone, Mia

numbly nodded, ran back to her cottage, stuffed Harper's swim stuff into a bag then arrived back at the gazebo in about two minutes flat.

She watched the happy trio saunter off down the hill. Then, her body bristling with irritation, she turned to Brin, who was straightening a pile of 'Sun Smart' flyers. 'Brin, we put the leaflets here, not there.' She picked up the leaflets and put them on the opposite side of the table.

His nostrils flared but he nodded. 'Sorry. I thought I was helping.'

'I said she couldn't go swimming.' Her irritation had got the better of her, or maybe it was nerves.

He put his hands up in surrender. 'Hey, I didn't say she could.'

'No, but you said it was hot. Which kind of meant she should go cool off.' She didn't know why she was so irked about this.

'I didn't say she should get wet. I'm sorry if you think I overstretched.'

'I've spent the whole of her life making decisions with her and for her. I'm not used to someone else having an opinion. Or, at least, voicing one.'

'I'm sorry. I understand.' He came a little closer and put his hand on her arm. And why, oh why, did it make her heart jump for joy when it should have been hardening against him? 'Hey, this isn't about Harper, is it?' he crooned in his gorgeous accent. 'You've been tetchy all morning.'

She felt a little called out. 'I have not.'

But he didn't rise to her irritation. He laughed. He laughed! 'Mia, you have been Miss Grumpy all morning. At least, with me. "Brin, we put the leaflets here, not there",' he said in an almost perfect imitation of Mia's voice and words. And she had to admit she'd been...*picky* this morning. But she was confused. She didn't know how to act around him in front of Owen or her daughter. Not when all she wanted to do was sink into another kiss with him. Her voice was always high-pitched when she talked to him, her breath always thready. She wasn't her usual calm and composed self. He *got* to her.

Brin sighed and ran his palm down her arm, making her want to curl into his embrace instead of rebuild her emotional barriers. 'Look, I know we overstepped with the kiss and everything. And I apologise.'

She shrugged away from his touch in case she did something stupid, like snuggle against him. 'Do we have to talk about this?'

The smile hadn't left his mouth. 'We do. Yes. Otherwise it'll be buzzing around in my head. If I deal with it, it'll go.'

She couldn't help smiling at this admission. 'So, you too?'

'Yep. I can't stop thinking about it and how

much I'd like to do it again. But I know it's not good for us. Or for Harper. She's the most important person in all of this.'

That was one thing they could agree on, at least. 'Exactly what I was thinking.'

'So, can we put it behind us?'

I'd like to do it again.

Me too.

She didn't know if she could put all these weird feelings behind her, but she nodded. 'Yes.'

'Good. Normal service is resumed.' He inhaled, then exhaled slowly.

'Can I have some sunscreen, please?' Lochie Taylor, from Harper's nursery, thrust out his hand. Mia squirted some into it, then made sure he was thoroughly covered. A hooter sounded and a roar came up from the crowds.

The race was on.

'Thanks!' Lochie tore away from her and ran towards his mum on the crowded jetty, and Mia watched as he ran between the legs of an elderly lady, sending her flying onto the concrete road.

'Whoa!'

'Got it,' Brin called as he ran to help the woman, who wasn't moving. Lochie looked horrified, so Mia rushed over to find his mum in the throng. By the time she arrived back, Brin had the lady sitting up on the ground, saying, 'Hey, now, Marion love—don't you be moving yourself until we've looked at the damage.'

She had a lump and bruising over her right temple, but nothing else. He looked up, caught Mia watching him, smiled and gave her a thumbs-up.

Mia nodded, knowing Marion was in safe hands. She'd felt the security in those hands herself; the safety and solace he provided, along with a whole lot more.

He wasn't easily ruffled. Except, she recalled, when she'd stepped on to the helicopter, and during every moment alone with her since. He wasn't ruffled around Harper, he was a pushover. He wasn't ruffled around Owen, or anyone else. Mia shook her head. Maybe he was just ruffled around her. That made her belly tighten. Because she was definitely ruffled around him, whether she wanted to be or not. 'I'll grab some ice.'

'Great. And we'll walk slowly over to the chair, eh, Marion?'

They managed to get her into a chair, took her blood pressure and put some ice on her bump. They calmed her down and called her relatives, who were in another bay, waiting for the race to come through.

Brin popped inside to get Marion a glass of water and, as she drank it, Mia took him to one side. 'If you want to have a wander round or watch the race, feel free. I can manage on my own.'

He frowned. 'I'm fine here.'

'But it's your day off. I feel bad you're working when you came here for a rest.'

'I came to see you.' His gaze latched on to hers and she felt the enormity of what he was saying. He'd come to make amends. To do his best. To get to know his daughter. And Mia had kissed him and then snapped at him. But he smiled. 'It's hardly taxing work. I'll tell you what—when we're done here, you can show me around the place.'

'Okay. Deal.' She laughed. 'It won't take long— it's not exactly a huge place. Once Harper's done playing with Mason, we'll take you for a tiki tour.'

'Excellent.' He gave a sharp nod and started back towards their patient with a quick, 'It's a date.'

It's a date.

Her belly fluttered. She knew it was just a turn of phrase and, especially after what they'd agreed, she knew it didn't mean anything. But part of her was excited about the prospect of spending more time with him…for Harper's sake. A platonic relationship between parents who were friends was a good thing.

They were interrupted by someone with a blister, then a child with a grazed knee, someone with hay fever and another with a heat rash. All of this took up the next hour, which flew by very quickly, yet at the same time seemed to stretch and stretch—usually coinciding with Mia thinking about the 'date'.

As Marion's relatives finally led her away, with strict instructions from Brin to take her to her GP back on the mainland later this afternoon, Mia's phone rang: Carly. Even though Mia knew that there was bound to be nothing wrong, her heart still stuttered. Ever since the day she'd lost her family to the sea, she panicked at personal calls. 'Hi, Carly. What's up?'

Carly's voice was light. 'Hey! The kids are happily building sandcastles and I've said they can stay a while longer. Why don't you pick Harper up later?'

Mia glanced at Brin, who was starting to tidy away the things on the table. 'I'm fine to collect her as soon as we've finished packing up here.'

'It's all good, honestly. Mason will only complain that he's bored if she goes home. Take the afternoon off.'

Show Brin around on her own…? 'It's okay, I'll be over soon.'

'Well, I have her now. She's my niece and I'm not giving her back until later.' Carly chuckled and Mia knew there was definitely a little meddling going on here. 'When was your last child-free afternoon?'

Mia thought. 'When we went to Auckland to sign the sale of the camp.'

'Exactly. We didn't even get to spend the night there before flying back here, and you've worked non-stop ever since. It's only a few hours. Have fun.'

'Carly—'

'Love you. Bye.'

Carly had gone before Mia had a chance to answer. Damn it—she couldn't hide behind her daughter now. She was going to have to show him around the island on her own.

'It's a date.' *Eejit.*

They'd decided they weren't going to act any further on their undeniable attraction and then he'd said the 'D' word. What was it about Mia that made him reckless and impulsive?

She looked gorgeous today, in a pink-and-white gingham sundress. Her blonde hair was tied back into a ponytail, her skin was fresh and make-up-free and she looked impossibly pretty and younger than her thirty-two years.

'A boat?' He blinked as she walked him to the jetty. He followed her down a ramp and onto a white fibreglass motorboat. He didn't know much about boats, but this looked well-loved, with its two padded seats, navy-blue canopy, bow rails, space for fishing rods and storage.

She grinned at him. 'How else do we get round an island?'

'By foot?'

'We are literally going *round* the island, Brin. Sit down and hold on.' She gunned the engine and the boat juddered as she steered it out of the marina towards open water. She was confident and obviously very experienced in handling the boat.

They turned right out of the harbour and then into a smaller bay, where the water was so clear he could see large stingrays slithering along the ocean bottom. There was a tiny sandy beach and a smattering of buildings dotted on a bush-lined hill. He didn't know the names of all the native New Zealand trees but could identify ferns and palm trees. Moored boats bobbed in the bay and seabirds dive-bombed the water to catch the myriad silver fish he saw darting beneath the surface.

Mia killed the engine and sighed. 'This is one of my favourite bays. It's so peaceful and there's shelter from the wind.'

'It's gorgeous.'

She pointed to a little cottage near the shore. 'That's Owen and Mason's place. Carly's too, now, I imagine.'

He frowned. 'They're together? Of course they're together—I saw them at the camp after the storm.'

'Carly was going to go overseas but she decided to stay here with Owen.' Mia peered at the beach then at the cottage. 'They must have finished playing and gone inside. Never mind, I'll pop back later.'

'Nice place, but it's a bit isolated.' There were few roads on the island, he'd learnt, but every house had beach access and a boat.

She looked at him and her eyes narrowed. 'It's only a few minutes round to the yacht club from here. Their neighbours are just over the hill. But, yes, the island is a long way from anywhere.'

'Not sure I could live somewhere so far from a cinema and pubs and…life. You have to be very organised, right? Can't forget a pint of milk and pop back for one.'

'Really?' She shook her head. 'You couldn't imagine living here? It's beautiful.'

'Remotely beautiful.'

She frowned. 'It's a good life. The yacht club has a little store off to the side where they stock essentials, and the Mansion House has open-air movie nights in the summer. But the remoteness is why we're such a tight community here. We need each other's help. That's also why Owen and I take it in turns to be on call every other night. If someone needs something, we have to give them a hand, no matter what.'

If he'd been in any doubt, he now knew she was utterly committed to this place and its people. 'What do you do with Harper if you get called out?'

'To be fair, it's a rarity, but Anahera babysits. She's round in North Bay, so it's not too far.'

'You drive the boats at night?' He tried to hide his naïvety but clearly failed.

She laughed, her eyes shining in amusement. 'Of course. We have lights, Brin. It is the twenty-first century.'

'I've got a lot to learn.'

She'd kicked off her sandals and stood barefoot at the wheel, wind tugging wisps of her ponytail free. The breeze played with the hem of her dress, every now and then lifting the fabric to reveal a glimpse of her gorgeous legs.

The memory of that kiss slammed into his brain. His body prickled and he had to force himself to walk to the other end of the boat before he reached for her again.

Luckily, she restarted the engine and the cool breeze and the hull skidding over the waves distracted him. Not enough, but some.

Next, they visited the outdoor camp with its huge red *SOLD* sticker across the Camp Rāwhiti sign. It looked a completely different place from what he remembered of a few days ago. His impression had been of panicked people, pain and shock. But now it looked pretty, with scarlet-flowered flax bushes and blue agapanthus lining the gravel paths. The boat shed was locked up, but he imagined school kids playing about on the water in little boats with white sails.

Back from the beach, the main camp building dominated the space. It was two-storey with the kitchen-diner at the front, where he'd spent the uncomfortable night trying to work out who Mia was. And there was the little annexe higher up the hill behind the main block, where he'd learnt that Harper was his daughter.

As they drew closer, he noticed Mia became quieter. Her shoulders slumped forward and she stared at the buildings with haunted eyes. Jeez, he had enough memories of this place to last him a few years, but she had a lifetime of them. Of growing up, losing her family and giving birth, all here in this little bay.

He wanted to slide his arm around her shoulder and give her comfort but thought better of it. They'd agreed not to kiss, so touching her was far too much temptation. 'So, you sold the camp?'

'We did. Carly and I.' She shrugged, then slowed the boat and steered towards the jetty.

'Do you mind me asking why?'

'Carly wanted to travel, and the camp needed renovating. I couldn't do it, not with my job and little Harper to look after.'

'It's a lot of work.' Her life would have been simpler if he'd been aware of Harper's existence. He could have helped, shouldered some of the burden.

'Now it's someone else's problem.' She looked towards the wooden buildings as she wrapped her arms tight round her chest, looking every bit as if it were still her problem.

'I was talking about working and looking after a child being hard.'

She blinked. 'I love my job and my daughter. I can do both.'

'I have no doubt. I'm not judging you. Just acknowledging how hard it's been for you. Is the new owner going to keep it as a camp?'

'Last thing we heard, there were plans to turn it into some kind of fancy resort.' This shrug was filled with sadness.

'How do you feel about that?'

'Weird. I know it's just bricks and mortar, and I thought I was okay with it. But I do feel guilty. Maybe I should have tried harder to keep it going in my parents' memory.' She rubbed her palms up and down her arms. 'It was their life's work. When I'd thought about selling the place, I'd been wooed by the prospect of a good future for me and Harper, but actually signing on the dotted line made me rethink. Too late now, of course. But sometimes I worry I've sold their memory down the river so I can have a new kitchen.'

If only she'd found him earlier, he might have been able to spare her this kind of worry. 'Harper is my daughter too. I'll help you out financially, obviously.'

She turned to look at him. 'I can't even think about that right now.'

No. This was all about her grief and some misplaced guilt. 'When my mam died, I felt the same. Like, how do I keep her memory alive?'

'What did you do? I have a bench with their names on, which we concreted into the ground by the playground. I've asked the new owner if I can have it and I've got permission to put it next to the marina. But do you think I should do something else?' The boat rocked under the swell of the waves, and she reached for a rail to steady herself. In the wispy dress, and with the haunted look in her eyes, she looked so vulnerable it made his chest hurt.

Without second-guessing himself, he put his hand on her shoulder. Felt her warmth under his fingertips. 'You'll keep your family alive in stories you tell Harper. You are testament to them. Your parents' legacy is inside you, Mia. In everything you do, how you treat people, who you are.'

'Not *everything* I do, I hope. I've made a few poor choices.' She smiled but still looked thoughtful.

'You mean me? That night?' He laughed. But he also knew there was a part of his father and brother inside him too. People didn't just inherit the good DNA.

She put her hand on his chest. 'Oh, Brin. It was a good night. Just with a complicated outcome.'

'A beautiful one.'

'Yes.' She smiled and it was as if she'd been dipped in sunshine, glowing in the soft light. His chest felt cracked open, just looking at her and thinking of everything she'd been through.

The moment lengthened as they looked at each other. The memory of last night's kiss seeped into his brain. She was so close…

He ran his fingers over her jaw.

Her eyes misted.

One kiss. How easy would it be to give in? To lean into the feeling, to take what they both wanted?

Her mouth opened slightly and her tongue dipped out and wetted her lower lip.

He ran his thumb there.

She gasped.

One kiss.

A bird squawked overhead, breaking the moment. He could not be lured in by the fact she'd asked his opinion about something so deeply personal. Or by the fact he'd never seen anyone or anything as beautiful as she was in this moment. He couldn't deepen this connection.

He stepped back and cleared his throat, hoping to clear the blurring in his head. 'Um, you don't mind being on boats after everything that happened?'

She stepped away too, as if realising this increased intimacy wasn't a great idea. 'I've got the ocean in my veins, Brin. I don't have the option of liking or not liking boats. This island is my home and boating is the quickest way to get from A to B. Besides, it's a beautiful day, and we're only going round the headland, so I reckon we're okay. Hold on.'

She turned and restarted the boat engine. The moment was gone.

But, no matter how much he tried, the need he felt for her still lingered.

CHAPTER EIGHT

MIA PULLED UP into the next bay and breathed out. Being this close to Brin was not good for her. The gentle way he spoke, the way he listened and answered her questions so honestly, made her feel seen and heard. Made her believe she was doing the right things, making the right decisions in her life. It was good to have that validation. Empowering.

Except the decision to kiss him last night—and again just now, when she'd almost given in—was not a wise decision at all. She had to stay strong. Maybe at the end of this weekend he'd leave and never come back and she'd be right back where she'd started: a solo mum with a lovely daughter and just a little bit lonely.

But that was okay. She'd been fine being that person. She didn't need upheaval. And, even if she craved them, she didn't *need* kisses from a gorgeous man with a sexy accent and good heart. She couldn't risk any more heartbreak in her life.

She moored up and climbed the steps to the

jetty, aware he was following her and unsure if she could keep her cool around him much longer. So she adopted a tour-guide role and pointed to the magnificent white two-storey colonial building on the reserve. It had wide verandas and filigree ironwork on the railings. 'This is the Mansion House. Built in the eighteen-hundreds for one of the first governor generals in New Zealand.'

He looked impressed. 'Very fancy.'

'Indeed. There are peacocks around somewhere and there used to be olive groves out the back. And monkeys and zebras, apparently.'

'Wow. You wouldn't expect that in a place like this.'

'It's not the right environment for them. I think only the peacocks are left now. But…' she grinned, pointing towards the café '…the best thing about this place is the home-made ice-cream.'

'Now you're talking my language.' He laughed and ran towards the café, the way Harper might have. The way Mia might have, once upon a time, before the weight of everything had crushed her. Sometimes, she thought, she'd forgotten how to have fun.

They sat in the sunshine on the reserve eating their ice-creams and watched as a ferry docked and a small group of teenagers piled onto the jetty.

Brin turned to her. 'I've realised I have no idea about so much of your island life. What do the kids here do for school?'

'We have a small primary over the hill there.' She pointed towards Jackson's Point round the headland. 'The older kids can choose to board on the mainland, do correspondence school or home school.'

'What did you do?' He licked a drip of strawberry ice-cream from his fingers. She watched hungrily, remembering the amazing things he'd done with that tongue. With those fingers. Heat suffused her skin.

She swallowed. 'My parents home-schooled us. We were around other kids all the time anyway, so we didn't miss out on the social side. Plus, there are plenty of families here now. Anahera's kids were and still are some of my best friends.'

'What do you think we'll do for Harper?'

We.

Warmth spread through her at the way he'd embraced his new role. She'd never had to discuss these things with anyone so totally invested in Harper's life, because she'd always been the sole decision-maker where her daughter was concerned. Sure, Carly, Anahera and other friends gave opinions but, in the end, the decision was always hers to make.

She suddenly turned cold. Now she'd be sharing making these decisions with Brin. But, despite their amazing chemistry, she didn't know him well enough to trust him, did she? Not really. They'd known each other for a matter of hours. He didn't know Harper, her strengths, or what kind of schooling would suit her needs. 'The primary here is as good as any I know in Auckland. Once she gets to year eight, we'll discuss options. Where did you go to school?'

'Dublin.'

'Did you like it?'

He crunched the rest of his cone, swallowed then leaned back on his elbows. 'I loved school. Loved learning things. I was captain of the football team and the chess club. You?'

'I aced maths and English. Got a few medals for dancing.'

'So, she's got grace, music and intellect on her side.'

Mia smiled, relenting. She knew her daughter better than anyone else. She would discuss the future, but she would very much advocate what she thought was best and make sure that happened. 'She's very clever. Loves reading… I guess you'd call it *practising* reading. She can recite all the stories, and knows if you're missing bits out so you can hurry story time up—'

Any further thought was cut short by the sound of a high-pitched scream.

* * *

Brin scrambled upright and ran towards the commotion, Mia tight at his heels. The kids were pointing into the water.

'What's happened?' Brin asked.

One of the kids turned to him, pale. 'Logan's fallen off the jetty.'

They looked to where he was pointing and saw a boy wedged between the jetty and the ferry, his face just about out of the deep water, and moaning in pain.

Brin peered down. 'Hey, Logan. I'm a paramedic. My name's Brin. There's some steps over there—can you swim over and climb out?'

'No,' Logan moaned.

'Did you hit something when you fell in? What hurts?'

The boy grimaced, raising his chin above the water as it lapped close to his mouth. 'My foot… it's stuck in something.'

'Oi! Grab this rope and I'll pull you out,' the ferry skipper shouted as he threw a swim-float attached to rope towards him, then side-mouthed to Brin, 'Bloody kids, messing about.'

'Let's get him out first,' Brin huffed. 'Then you can read him the riot act.'

'Stuck…' Logan's voice was muffled as water lapped into his mouth. He'd grasped the slippery, seaweed-covered jetty post but was struggling to keep his head above the waterline. 'Help me.'

'Grab the float.' The skipper's annoyance was laced with panic. 'Can you wriggle free? Is it reeds? Rope? What?'

'I don't know…' Logan's breath came fast as he coughed. The float bobbed on the top of the waves then got caught in the swell and swept away to the right, out of Logan's reach.

The skipper hauled the float back in and threw it again. It got caught between the ferry's hull and the jetty and lodged there, unusable.

Logan began to shake, kicking his legs. 'Help me.'

'Hey, man. Try to stay calm.' Heart jumping, Brin peered into the murky water, trying to see what was pinning Logan down.

The boy pressed tight back against the side of the jetty as the ferry loomed close, undulating in the waves. There were only a few inches or so between boat and boy.

'Move the ferry,' Brin ordered the skipper. 'Or he's going to get crushed.'

'My—my foot…' Logan started to splutter as water filled his mouth. 'Caught. Stuck. Can't move.'

Or he's going to drown.

'Wait. If you start the engine, he could drown in the wash.' Mia was by Brin's side, her hand on his back. Her touch was a comfort.

The skipper knelt and looked at the water, his face red and blotchy. 'It's not high tide yet but the tide's coming in. We need to get his foot free before he drowns.'

'Well, I'm not waiting.' Brin whipped off his T-shirt and dived into the water just beyond the boat's stern. Visibility was poor, as the ferry had disturbed the silt and sand, and Logan's kicking had made the water turbulent. Above him he could see light and shapes but down here, nothing.

Need air.

When he surfaced, he saw Mia kneeling at the edge of the jetty trying to hold Logan's head above the rising water. She looked calm as she talked to the boy, but he knew how much this must be affecting her. She'd said the water was part of her blood, but it had cruelly taken her family too.

No more. Not on his watch.

He dived down again. Peering hard, he made out some old rope attached to the side of the jetty. Somehow Logan's foot had become tangled and the more he writhed the more stuck he became.

Damn.

Brin kicked to the surface, trying not show the worry he felt to Logan or Mia. 'His foot is caught on some rope, and we need to cut him free. We need space.' Brin touched Logan's shoulder. 'I need you to stop…stop kicking, mate. Please.'

Mia called to a deck hand. 'Knife! Get me a knife. Quickly.'

It felt like for ever until the deck hand returned and passed the knife to Mia. She handed it down to Brin. 'Here you go.' Her eyes were dark and her face pale. She was trembling and stretching to hold Logan's face out of the water. But she nodded and gave him a small smile. 'You've got this, Brin. But please, be careful. We... Harper needs you to be okay.'

His daughter's name galvanised him. Brin's heart hammered against his rib cage. He wasn't a great swimmer. He didn't know what he was going to do if he couldn't cut the rope. And he most certainly didn't know if he'd *got* anything, let alone the capability to hold his breath long enough to get this boy free. But he was damned well going to prove Mia's belief in him. This boy was someone's child. He nodded to her, hauled in more air then dived back down.

The rope was gnarly and old but thick. He grabbed Logan's foot to stop him kicking, and so he wouldn't cut the lad. But Logan was scared, the water was rising and he was kicking for his life.

Brin scraped the knife against the rope. It barely made a scratch. The knife wasn't sharp enough. The rope too thick. It was going to take longer than he'd thought.

Do it, man. This is someone's child.

He'd want someone to do this for his kid if they were in danger. He'd want someone to go above and beyond. With the image of little Harper at the forefront of his mind, Brin cut, cut and cut. But it wasn't working. With the water and the blunt serrations, it wasn't working.

His lungs burned and his desperate need for air forced him back up. He broke the surface, panting and coughing.

Mia's face screwed up in torment. 'Brin?'

'I can't… It's not…' He greedily gulped snatches of air as his words taunted him.

I can't.

Not good enough.

Someone's child. Someone's son.

That was not how this was going to play out. He gulped more air into his lungs and dived back down into the murky water. He angled the knife and sawed and sawed, putting all his strength into each action. Some of the rope began to fray but not enough.

Come on! Come on!

Next to him Logan's kicking started to slow. Was he drowning? Was it too late?

No.

No!

Brin's chest was on fire.

Air. Need air.

He kicked up to the surface and saw the boy's mouth barely above the water. 'Logan, hold on, man. Hold on.'

Mia's face crumpled. 'Brin, please.'

Please...what? Stop? Try harder?

He couldn't let this boy die and then go back to his little girl and be the man he wanted to be, knowing he hadn't done everything, given everything.

He dived back down. Sawed and sawed and sawed and sawed.

Come on...come on!

Suddenly, the rope sprang apart. Logan's foot was free and disappearing up and out of the water.

Brin's lungs were screaming, his thoughts blurring. But he managed to grab hold of the jetty post and clawed his way up into beautiful fresh air. 'Is—is he okay?' he choked out.

'He's...he's coughing. But he's okay. He's safe up here.' Mia offered him her hand and pulled him up out of the water. Her eyes were glistening and her smile was sweet with relief. 'I thought... Oh, Brin. Thank you.'

She wrapped her arms round him and pressed her face against his chest, her whole body trembling. He held her the way he had that night and stroked her back. 'Hey, it's okay. It's okay.'

He imagined how she must have felt when she'd watched him dive down over and over again, wondering if he'd resurface. Her life and her losses were inextricably connected to the sea.

'Brin, please.'

Her voice had been laced with distress. For

Logan or for him? Had she been reliving that tragedy all over again?

She eased back and shook her head, her eyes haunted. 'I'm so glad you're okay.'

'Yeah. Me too.' He wanted her back in his arms but knew the hug had probably been a friend-to-friend, relief kind of hug and nothing more. So instead he bent to look at the boy. His ankle was red from rope burns and he was pale, shaking and coughing. Someone had wrapped him in a towel and there was a huddle of concerned adults round him. 'You okay, Logan?'

'I'm...good.' The boy looked up at him and shook his head. 'Thanks. I thought... I thought I was going to drown.'

'Yeah, I was worried too.' Brin's chest was hurting and he couldn't quite catch his breath properly. 'But all we got was a bit wet, right? And a sore foot. But you'll live to fight another day.'

Logan gave him a weak smile. 'I'm going to watch where I walk in future.'

'Good lad.' Brin tousled the kid's hair. Then he turned and found Mia looking at him, holding his T-shirt tight to her chest and wearing a strange expression that he couldn't quite name.

Mia was still shaking by the time they got back to her boat. She grabbed a towel and threw it over Brin's shoulders. 'I thought... You were down there a long time.'

'The rope was so thick, it took a bit of effort to cut it.' He shook his head and started to rub his chest dry.

He said thick without the *'h'*: *'t'ick'*. It was desperately sexy and cute, and made her want him even more, but she was shaken by the strength of her panic when he'd dived into the water. Then, when he hadn't surfaced for such a long time, she'd prayed and hoped he'd be okay. It was like a rerun of her life: the worst bits, the waiting. Only this time it had been minutes, not days.

He'd been prepared to risk his life for someone he didn't know. But then, that was his job. He cared for people; he looked out for them, looked after them. He saved them. As did she. She might not fully trust him with her heart, but she understood him, saw his motivation to help and felt it resonate deep inside her. If he'd do that for someone else's child, what would he be prepared to do for his own? He wouldn't walk away, surely?

'Okay, big-shot hero, let's get you back to the B and B so you can get some dry clothes on.' She inhaled on a shiver, and he must have noticed, because he stopped rubbing and looked at her.

'You okay?'

'Not really.' She felt shaken, turned on and anxious all rolled into one. She *liked* him, so that made everything worse, and now she realised she cared about him. Cared for him. Just how much after such a short time, she wasn't prepared to explore.

She flicked the key, started the boat engine and steered slowly out of the bay, homeward bound. What could she do with all these feelings inside her? It was overwhelming. 'I was worried about you, Brin.'

'Really?' He sidled up next to her and grinned. 'Well, that's nice.'

'Nice? I thought you were going to drown or get crushed. *Nice?*'

'Fortunately, I'm very much uncrushed, although slightly damp.' But his grin was replaced with something more serious. 'Look, Mia, I know how you must have been feeling. I'm sorry if it brought back bad memories.'

'It did. But I'm okay, thanks. You rescued Logan and you're alive, and my concern is apparently *nice.*' She couldn't help laughing then, because it was such an underwhelming word to describe everything she was feeling.

He winked at her and spread his arms as if to say, *here I am.* 'If you don't like nice, would you prefer naughty?'

Giggling, she flicked her hand at him. 'Not with you, Brin O'Connor. Get away from me.'

But he'd made her laugh and the tension of the last few minutes ebbed away. How could she go from panicked to laughter so easily?

Brin—that was why. She sneaked a quick

glance at him as he rubbed down his legs. The last few years had been good to him. It wasn't only his face that was tanned. His whole body was gorgeously sun-kissed. He worked out, that much was obvious, had strong, toned arms, a solid wall of abdominal muscle and a smattering of dark hair arrowing from his belly button... down.

She turned away...and looked back.

She turned away again. A movement in the water to her left had her peering closer. She stopped the engine.

Brin frowned. 'What's the matter?'

'I wanted to show you...' She pointed to a group of little blue-and-cream birds in the water, diving and swimming. 'Little blue penguins.'

His eyes lit up as he watched the tiny birds. 'They're incredible. Great little divers. I could get some tips from them.'

She smiled, glad of the distraction from him and all these feelings. 'They're so cute. The smallest penguins in the world. They nest over there in the bay, up the hill a little in burrows and tree roots.'

'They nest up the hill? Not on the beach?'

'Mostly up in the scrubby areas. They waddle up at night and then back down here for food and a swim in the morning.'

'Sounds like my kind of life—swimming and snacks.' He chuckled.

She laughed too. 'You don't waddle.'

'I could.' He dropped the towel and wiggled his backside with his arms straight by his sides, a poor but funny impression of a penguin.

She giggled. 'Well, I'll drop you off over in the bay and you can go waddle with your mates.'

'I think I've got wet enough for one day, *thanks*.' He rubbed the towel across his hair. Then he stopped and looked at her, his eyes softening. 'Mia, really, thank you.'

Her heart thrummed. 'For…?'

'This day. Showing me the island. The penguins, the Mansion House, your favourite bay… It's been more than I hoped for.'

She tried to wave him off with nonchalance. 'You need to know where your daughter lives.'

'And now I can picture her here when I'm back in the city in my apartment.'

He was really smitten. And, even though she knew he was only smitten with their daughter and not with her island, she felt a sliver of hurt spear her heart at his absolute intention to leave. 'Rāwhiti is a good place to live. She loves it here.'

'It's very different to what I'm used to, that's for sure.' His eyebrows rose. 'And thanks, Mia, for giving me a chance. Getting to know me.'

'It's important, you know, for Harper. I needed to make sure you're trustworthy and reliable.' She had to detach from her own feelings about him.

He was going back to Auckland. He did not want to live here.

But, oh, it was more than that. She'd watched him dive into the water and prayed he'd come back up. He'd been down there so long, she'd thought… She couldn't lose another person to the ocean. When he'd surfaced, her heart had been so full, she'd wanted to wrap him in her arms and hold him. To be sufficiently freed up in her heart to be able to take what she wanted and not worry about losing him.

'And?' He smiled, waiting for her judgement of him. 'Am I? Trustworthy and reliable?'

She shook her head. 'The jury is still out.'

'Looks like I've got my work cut out to prove myself.'

'We've a long way to go yet, Brin.' She looked away, knowing her confusion and desire must be mirrored on her face.

But he touched her arm, bringing her to face him again. 'I get it. I do. And this…seeing you again after all this time…it's unreal, Mia.'

'Brin…' It was meant to be a warning, but it was more like a sigh. Or a prayer. *Brin.* How many times had she sobbed his name over the years, wondering where he was? Wishing he'd been here…when she'd seen the two blue lines on the pregnancy test. When she'd thrown up in those early months. When she'd held their baby for the first time she'd whispered his name into her daughter's perfect little ears, hoping that by some miracle she'd find him and show him what they'd made. When Harper had been sick and Mia had been at her wits' end. When she'd been exhausted from breastfeeding. When Harper had taken her first steps.

Brin.

He smiled. 'This is all… I didn't expect. Didn't think… I don't know. It's a lot.'

'It is.' It was too much—his closeness, his smile, the gentle look in his eyes as they talked about Harper. The hope—yes, the hope that things might be a little bit better, now he was back.

He was so close…and there was an expanse of broad chest that looked so inviting she ached to put her head there and breathe him in.

She closed her eyes, trying to fight the need rushing through her.

'Mia?' His breath whispered over her cheek. 'What's wrong?'

'Nothing. Everything. I…' She opened her eyes, barely able to breathe, the desperation to touch him so overwhelming, it suffused her whole body. 'Is it weird that we only had one night together but I missed you for the next few weeks?'

'Months?' He spoke at the same time as her. He chuckled. 'If you're weird, then I am too.'

She looked into his eyes and saw that he meant it. He'd missed her the way she'd missed him.

But she'd lied. She'd missed him for the last three years.

'I never forgot you.' His gaze slid to her mouth. 'I couldn't get you out of my head. That night, Mia…'

Her heart drummed against her chest bone. 'We can't…shouldn't…'

He opened his arms, hands palm-up, and shrugged.

Your choice. Your move.

And, oh, she couldn't resist—just a hug, not a kiss. She stroked her fingertips down his bare chest, walked into his open arms, rested her head against his shoulder and held him.

It felt… Oh, *God*. It felt so good to be right there in his arms, skin on skin. Heat skittered through her, and she felt the fast beat of his heart against her chest. She ran her fingers up his arms, stroking his soft skin, running over the swell of his biceps. She felt him shudder in pleasure. He pressed his forehead to hers, closing his eyes and inhaling a shaky breath. His movements were slow…too slow…but the power and sensuality of his touch had her fizzing with desire.

He cupped the back of her neck, then traced forward over her shoulder, skimming her décol-letage, and lower, until his fingers grazed her nipples over her dress. He ran his knuckles over them, then palmed her breast, watching her reaction. No doubt *feeling* her reaction as her nipples beaded.

'Brin.' She gasped and her eyes fluttered closed, savouring his touch.

'Mia… Mia…' He rubbed his forehead against hers, then pressed his mouth to her cheek. 'Mia.'

'Yes. Yes.' She turned her head and his mouth was there, his head tilted towards her, and there was no way she could stop this. She angled her head and he touched his lips to hers.

It was a whisper of a kiss, a feather's touch. But it set her aflame.

'Brin.' She moaned as she wound her arms round his neck and tugged him closer, pressing all of her against all of him. She slid her mouth over his. He tasted of the sea, salt and fresh air. Of something so intensely elemental and sensual, she couldn't get enough.

He pressed her against the seat, his hardness hot against her core as he opened his mouth to kiss her with the same hunger she felt. She raked her hands across his back, urging him closer, pulsing against his erection.

He slid his hands down her legs and grasped the hem of her dress, bunching it up her thighs, his caress rough and desperate. His fingers traced the inside of her thigh, a tease she couldn't bear. Because she wanted him inside her.

She angled her legs until his fingers flicked the hem of her panties, stroking her centre.

'God, Mia. I need to be—'

Honk!

From somewhere behind them, a horn sounded and, through eyes barely able to focus, she whirled round to see a flotilla of yachts sailing towards them.

Hot damn. The race!

She jumped away from him, wiping a trembling hand across her mouth. Bad enough that they'd given in to temptation again, but a whole fleet of sailors and friends had caught them at it. 'Quick! We're in the path of the race.'

She flicked the engine on and steered them out of the direct line. 'The finish is round that headland.'

He grinned and held on to the back of her seat. 'Caught out like naughty school kids.'

'It isn't funny,' she threw at him.

His eyes roamed her face, scrutinising her reaction, and his smile melted away. 'No. You're right. It isn't funny at all. It's actually very serious.'

'This is where I live, Brin. This is my home. I don't need them all knowing my private business. We need to stop this. You can see Harper, of course. But all this…us spending time together…it's not going to work. It's too much.

Too…everything.' And, with hands that would not stop shaking, she steered them home.

Who knew how far they might have gone if they hadn't been disturbed? Who knew how deep she'd have let herself fall when she needed to be vigilant around him? Twice today they'd been so intimate, it had made her thoughts blurry. She had to steel herself against him.

No kissing. No messing about in boats.

No falling for him.

Thank God the flotilla had arrived when it did.

CHAPTER NINE

'IS THERE ANYONE HERE? Please, help me.' A woman staggered through the clinic door, clutching her pregnant stomach. She had a nasty gash above her eye and was clearly shocked and breathless.

'Hey, sure.' Mia jumped up and helped the woman into her consulting room, where she plumped up the pillow and assisted her to climb onto the examination couch. 'My name's Mia. I'm the nurse-practitioner on the island. What's your name?'

'Ruth.' The woman looked down at palms which were grazed, gritty and bleeding.

'Looks like you've been through the wars. What's happened?'

'I tripped on the path and landed heavily on my side. Now I think I've started bleeding...down there. I don't know... I'm all wet, but I daren't look.' Tears shone in her eyes and worry nipped at her features. 'Is my baby okay?'

Mia knew how that worry felt. Carrying a baby

had been the most precious, wonderful and scary thing she'd ever done. Suddenly she was responsible for another life that depended utterly on her for everything. She made sure her tone was gentle and reassuring, even though placental abruption was her first and worrying thought. 'Okay, let's take a look. How far along are you?'

'Thirty-two weeks.'

'Your first?'

'Yes.' Ruth ran her hand over her swollen belly then her face creased in anguish. 'Oh. Oh…it hurts.'

Mia put her palm on Ruth's belly and felt the ripple under her fingers. 'Looks like the fall might have brought on early labour.'

Ruth grabbed Mia's hand tightly. 'Is there…a doctor here?'

'Usually, yes. But he's away for the next couple of days.' Owen had gone to the mainland for an emergency-management course, leaving Mia in sole charge, which was always a challenge, but one she relished. She'd completed extra courses over the years to equip her to handle most things that came her way.

Before Owen had arrived, she'd had to manage emergencies on her own. But, as the island population had grown, and therefore the demand, the community had decided they needed more than one medically trained expert, so had petitioned the powers that be to help provide one.

Mia held the woman's hand until the contraction had passed, all the while assessing her patient. 'You're doing great. I need to do an examination. Is that okay?'

'Yes, yes, please. Make sure my baby's okay.'

'First, I'll check baby's heartbeat.' Mia squeezed her hand, aware that every mum wanted to be reassured that all was well.

She lifted the Doppler from the drawer, squeezed jelly onto Ruth's bump and ran the transducer over her skin. The welcome sound of a quick heartbeat filled the air. Mia breathed out in relief, then went on to do the vaginal examination. 'What were you hoping for, for your birth care and plan?'

'I was going to stay with my mum on the mainland from next week, then go to the hospital from there.'

Mia pulled off her blood-stained gloves and threw them in the bin. Ruth was spotting but not haemorrhaging. The baby's heartbeat was normal but she still needed to get her to hospital as soon as possible. 'Well, you might have to be flexible. Your cervix is definitely softening, which usually means early labour. It's best we get you to hospital quickly so you can have a full examination and ultrasound. The doctors can give you something to slow things down or hopefully stop the contractions altogether, and they'll want to monitor you. We like to keep baby cooking for as long as we can.'

'But what if he comes soon? Will he be okay? He's very little.'

'Thirty-two weeks is early, yes, and he might need a little help once he's born, so we need to get you both the right care. The sooner the helicopter gets here, the better.'

'Okay. Should I go pack a bag or something?'

'Do you live here? I thought I knew everyone on the island.' But she'd been distracted the last couple of weeks and not paying attention to the comings and goings on her little island home. It was all because of Brin, course—the restless nights and daydreams, making her heart sore yet hopeful. Making her excited about a future with him in it and scared about how to navigate it all in the midst of such an intense and unsustainable attraction. After the boat kiss, she'd cried off any further communication that day and hidden at home, pretending to have a headache, so she wouldn't have to face him again.

Yes, she was a coward.

He'd been gone four days now and she'd received one text a day enquiring about how she and Harper were. She'd answered them all with politeness, trying to not let her desire infiltrate her thoughts and messaging.

Ruth nodded. 'We moved here a couple of

weeks ago. We're renovating over in Beth's Bay. But my husband's gone back to the city to tie up some loose ends and get some more supplies.'

'Okay. Well, I don't want you moving around too much. We need to keep you on bed rest until you've been properly assessed. I could ask our receptionist to go to your house and grab some of your things.'

'Please. There's a spare key in a plant pot to the left of the door.'

'No problem. And, while we're waiting, I'll clean up those grazes. And perhaps you'd like to call your husband, let him know what's happening? Or I could do that for you?'

'I'll call him. He'll be so worried.' Ruth's bottom lip wobbled. 'It's taken us so long to get pregnant—three rounds of IVF and a lot of anxiety.'

Mia's heart went out to the young woman. She gave her hand a squeeze. 'I understand completely. I'll go and call the helicopter, then I'll be right back.'

Mia left the room and took a deep breath. Luckily, when she'd gone into labour, she'd only been a couple of weeks early, with no risk to her baby and no one to else to worry about. She put the emergency evacuation request through and called Anahera, who was on her lunch break. Then she went back to stay with Ruth until the chopper arrived.

Of course, it was Brin who arrived twenty minutes later, along with another paramedic, Emma. Mia breathed a sigh of relief as he walked in, as if she didn't have to worry any more.

But that was weird. This was her job, and she did it every day. She could deal with the emotional fallout from the more intense or complicated situations. Only, things seemed easier when he was around. His ready smile and willingness to help were endearing and attractive.

But things became a lot more complicated when he was around too.

He breezed in, smiled at Mia then turned his attention to their patient. 'Hi there, I'm Brin, and this is Emma. We're here to transport you to Auckland Women's.'

'The…cavalry?' Ruth breathed through another contraction.

He grinned and jokily flexed his biceps. 'That's us. Right, what's been going on?'

Mia gave him the details and watched as he slid his hand over Ruth's and squeezed it, saying, 'What an adventure you've been having. Don't worry, we'll get you to the hospital safe and sound. Just need to put in a drip to keep you hydrated, and I've some pain relief if you need it.'

Ruth grimaced. 'Only when the contractions hit.'

'Oh, I've something in my bag of tricks for that, don't you be worrying.'

Ruth's shoulders relaxed as she smiled up at him, as if he were some sort of superhero. 'Thank you.'

'No worries. Let's get you and your precious cargo into the wheelchair, then we'll scoot you up to the chopper.' They assisted Ruth into the chair and Emma took hold of the wheelchair handle. 'I'll get her up there if you can bring the bags.'

'Right behind you.'

Brin watched them leave then turned to Mia, his expression guarded. 'Hey, how are you doing?'

Despite the frostiness between them, her heart fluttered. But a fluttering heart wasn't going to keep him at arm's length. She stepped away. 'I'm fine.'

His eyes narrowed, as if he was assessing her response. 'And Harper?'

'Fine, too. She's at kindy.'

'Right.' He smiled but there was something brittle about it. 'Look, I know things got heavy the other day, but we're bigger than that, right?'

'Of course.'

'I was thinking…wondering…whether you wanted to come over to spend some time with me in Auckland? You and Harper?'

Stupid, fluttering heart.

'Actually, I was thinking of coming over to the city next weekend. Work's starting on my house on Monday and I need to order some new tiles, soft furnishings and furniture. I don't like to do that online. I like to see the colours in person. So perhaps we could meet up, yes.'

'Grand. You're welcome to stay at mine. I've a spare room.'

'For Harper?' she clarified.

'Of course. You can have my room and there's a couch in the lounge I can sleep on.' His nod was quick and sharp, as if there'd never been any doubt about where Mia would sleep.

Just looking at him, at those vibrant blue eyes and strong arms, her body tilted towards him. But her head stayed strong. 'I've booked a hotel.'

'Okay.' He didn't argue or try to push the issue. He'd clearly had second thoughts about the wisdom of kissing too. 'Well, you could come over for food or something. I'd like Harper to come visit my place.'

Mia's gut tightened into a knot. 'Because she needs to get used to being with you, at your house?' She heard the tremor in her voice.

He nodded. 'It's early days, and I wouldn't want you or her to feel pressured in any way, but yes—I'd like to see her regularly. Get some sort of routine going. I mean, it's not always easy with shift work, but I can put in requests for regular days off.'

She'd imagined this happening. She knew that Brin would be keen to see his daughter whenever he could, as he was that kind of man. But she hadn't expected her gut to hollow out at the thought of not seeing her daughter every other weekend.

For the rest of her life.

She swallowed back her feelings, not wanting to show them. It was better for Harper to get to know her father than for Mia to keep her here, preventing her from having a relationship with blood family just because she didn't want to share. It didn't mean it didn't hurt, though.

She nodded and dug for a smile. 'Okay. We'll come over on Saturday morning.'

'We could take her to the zoo or something, in between the heavy shopping itinerary? Or I could look after her while you do the sofa buying stuff.'

Did he want sole charge for the afternoon? She imagined the two of them playing their hide-be-hind-the-blanket game, or eating ice-creams together, and felt excluded before it had even happened. 'I don't know how I feel about you having sole care of her. You don't know her little foibles and habits. Things are moving a bit too fast.'

'But they do have to move, Mia. I'm experienced…' He hesitated and frowned, shaking his head. 'A fast learner. And I've got two and a bit years of catching up to do. You have to see that.'

She did. But, oh, she was conflicted. And he seemed so unaffected by the fact they'd made out—twice. His focus was all about Harper. It was what they'd agreed and what she wanted, but she couldn't get over how being in his presence made her thoughts blur and her limbs turn to jelly.

His radio crackled and he pressed the button to reply. 'On my way, Em. Sorry. Be there in five. Okay, Mia, I've got to go. See you next week.' He leaned in and kissed her cheek. A chaste little peck, nothing other than a friendly gesture. Nothing at all like what her body craved. She turned instinctively at his touch, wanting that mouth on hers.

But he'd stepped away.

She inhaled, getting a whiff of his delicious scent, and breathed out slowly as she watched him dart out of the door. She called out to him, 'I'll let you know the ferry times.'

'Grand,' he called back, his hand raised in a wave.

Which left her even more confused. How could she be this emotionally invested in what he did, thought and wanted after such a short time? How could she survive the next few years, having him flit in and out of her life like this and not have more of him to herself?

How could she spend a weekend with this man and get out sane?

CHAPTER TEN

BRIN'S CHEST HURT as he waited for the ferry to dock on Saturday morning. He felt a whole load of excitement mixed with a good dollop of anxiety. He'd never been nervous around kids before and had been a natural, good father to Niamh. But truth was he wanted to be the best father for Harper and to have Mia see that. He wanted her to trust him, because they were going to be in each other's lives for a long time, now they shared Harper.

And yet, at the same time, he had this gnawing worry that it was all going to be snatched away from him at any moment. He was going to lose all over again. He felt cleaved in two—wanting to run into this, giving his full heart, but at the same time wanting to run away from it and keep his heart safe.

Because the last time when he'd been happy he hadn't been ready when the truth had come out. It had blindsided him, shaken the foundations of what he'd thought it was to be family—to be a brother, to be loved and to love. So, he had to be ready for the next time. He was not going to go let himself be lulled by the promise of happy families.

Would he always feel like this—that he could never fully lean into happiness for fear he was going to lose it? His jaw clenched. His brother and his ex had a lot to answer for.

His brother... How could anyone do something so horrific to his own kin?

He peered at the line of people streaming off the ferry, looking for Mia's pretty smile and his happy, chatty daughter. But as the stragglers at the back disembarked his heart folded in on itself.

They weren't here. They weren't coming. Mia had obviously changed her mind. She didn't trust him.

He pulled out his phone and checked his messages—none.

He took one last look. The deck hands were opening the gates for the next load of passengers to walk on board.

They weren't coming.

Déjà vu. A different daughter and a different woman, but the same gut-wrenching feelings. He swallowed back the hurt and turned to walk away. He'd been right not to get too invested; he'd have to work out parental access through more formal avenues. But she could at least have let him down gently.

'Brin!'

Whoa!

He turned to see Mia rushing towards him, dragging a holdall on wheels and carrying another bag over her shoulder while pushing a pushchair with Harper in it, kicking her legs and waving at him. Mia was wearing a white tank top, a pink silk skirt that fell just below her knees, white trainers and an anxious frown. His heart danced at the sight of them.

He was next to her before he could think and took the shoulder bag and holdall from her hands. He made sure not to kiss her cheek this time. Last time, he'd been too close to kissing her full on the lips. 'Hey, it's good to see you both.'

But Mia frowned. 'Were you leaving? Did you think we weren't coming?'

They'd been delayed, that was all. He should have had more faith in her. He'd misjudged her and jumped to conclusions instead of believing in her. 'Yes... No... I thought you might have changed your mind.'

'I'd have messaged you, silly. I don't *not* turn up. Missy needed the loo just at docking time—potty training.' She rolled her eyes with a smile. 'Got to take advantage of the moment.'

'Fun times. Don't worry, I totally understand. You have to carry a potty around everywhere you go and it's often a little unpredictable at first.' He grinned with relief and felt as silly as she'd called him. But old traits died hard. How many times had he waited outside the house, or at the bus station, or in a café to see Niamh, only for her mother not to bother bringing her? How many times had his heart been dashed, from hope and excitement to disappointment?

But Mia wasn't Grainne, his ex; he needed to remember that.

Harper had her arms out to be hugged, so he put down the bags again, unclipped the pushchair straps and whipped her up into his arms, kissing her cheeks. 'Hey, cheeky chops. How are you?'

'Bwin!' Harper patted his cheeks and beamed at him. 'Cheek chops.'

'Did you do a wee in the toilet?' he asked, oddly pleased to hear all about it.

'No.' Mia shook her head. 'But we will next time, right, Harper?'

'Yes, Mumma.' Harper wriggled to be put down, so he helped her back into the buggy and picked up the bags.

'These things take time, but you'll get the hang of it.'

'You seem to know a lot about potty training. Are you the Wee Whisperer?' Mia laughed and Brin's gut jolted. He had never wanted to talk about what had happened between his ex and him, and the complication of his brother, and he wasn't about to start. It wasn't as if Niamh was a part of his life now, or his brother. And he knew that hurt would radiate from him if he so much as mentioned anything, so why darken the mood?

He smiled at his daughter. 'Ah, no. Been reading up on toddler taming.'

'Nothing like being prepared.' Mia laughed, but she was looking at him as if she wanted to ask him a question but didn't know what to say. 'Although, nothing can prepare you for the terrible twos.'

'Don't listen to her. She doesn't know what she's saying. You're not terrible, so you're not! You're gorgeous.' He winked at Harper and walked them to his car. Mia had messaged about car seats, so he'd bought one to make life easier for when Harper was visiting. It got the smile of approval and a corresponding punch of pride in his solar plexus at not only doing something right for Harper, but impressing Mia too.

The journey to his place involved a lot of chattering, Harper telling him what she'd been doing at kindergarten and wanting a drink, then needing a real wee this time and stopping at the public loos, everyone cheering at her success. It was good to have her there as a distraction because having Mia so close was muddling his brain. He'd thought a few days' respite from her would ease his attraction to her but…no. His car now smelt of her delicious scent, that was a constant seduction, and his body prickled and heated every time he looked at her.

'Nice place,' Mia said breezily as they finally got to his first-floor apartment in Ōrākei, and nodded as she looked round, clearly impressed. 'Renting, right?'

He'd tried to make it as homely as possible, but it was probably still very much a bachelor pad. 'Yes. But I'm hoping to buy somewhere at some point.'

'You're planning on staying, then?'

Was he?

'I've no plans to leave.'

'Which isn't the same thing.' She peered at him, waiting for a clearer answer. But he didn't know what to say. Before Harper, he'd planned to stay in New Zealand for a couple of years then move on. But now...? His plans had been utterly derailed.

But he'd had plans before—family plans; a future and a life that he'd thought was complete and settled—and they'd been derailed too. Making more concrete plans seemed foolish. Who knew what other shocks and surprises might be around the corner?

He shrugged, not wanting to illuminate her any further. 'I'm here for the foreseeable. None of us knows what the future holds, right? Until a couple of weeks ago I wouldn't have imagined my life changing so drastically. But here we are.'

'Here we are.' She looked up at him and smiled warily. But he could see the softness in her gaze and the way she tried to shrug it off by blinking. She was as confused by all of this as he was. 'Want to show us round?'

'Won't take long.' He laughed. 'It's not the biggest of places.'

But it had a decent-sized lounge, a spotlessly clean kitchen, a master bedroom with *en suite* bathroom and a spare room. Pale grey walls and sleek lines. A couple of minutes later, they were standing in his spare room, which with permission from the landlady he'd painted soft pink.

Mia sighed as she took it all in—the white wooden bed, white toy box waiting to be filled and white bookcase. 'Oh, you've bought a big girl's bed too. Look, Harper.'

Mum and daughter both went to test the mattress in a fit of giggles.

Watching them playing in the space he'd created gave him a shot of pride right in the middle of his chest. 'I thought Harper could pick out her own duvet cover, but I bought one just in case.'

Mia patted the duvet. 'I think *Frozen* will work fine.'

'An easy bet. Most girls her age are *Frozen*-obsessed.'

'You know a lot about children, Brin. What's popular, how to potty train…'

Damn. He'd given too much away again. 'It's my job to. Got to find a way of distracting the little ones when they're in pain, right?'

'Oh, yes. Of course.' She tickled Harper's tummy until the toddler was rolling about and giggling. 'Is it still okay if we stay?'

'Sure. I got everything ready in case you wanted to. Or Harper fell asleep here or something.' His heart squeezed at the thought of getting involved in his daughter's bedtime routine, spending those precious moments together.

Mia smiled tentatively. 'Thanks. I...um...cancelled the hotel. Seemed silly to splash out on something so frivolous when we can bunk down here.'

'No bunking. You can have my room. I'll take the sofa.' He was thrilled to have the chance to read Harper a bedtime story for the first time in his life. But, hell, how was he going to cope with having Mia so close, in the next room?

All night...

She breathed out. 'Thanks. But I'm okay on the sofa, honestly.'

'My bed it is.' He tried not to look at her; he really did. But his gaze collided with hers and he couldn't miss the heat in her eyes, the flare of something. He imagined her in his bed, doing the things they'd done that one night together. Remembered the way she'd held him, gripped him, the way they'd fitted together so perfectly.

He swallowed back his reaction because they had to do this right. They couldn't keep falling into each other's arms. Couldn't allow their attraction to override sense. 'Right, we have things to do. Let's go shopping for…what was it…tiles? Sofas?'

Mia picked Harper up from the bed and followed him back into the lounge. 'Maybe tomorrow. Perhaps we can go to Kelly Tarlton's today?'

'The aquarium place down the road?'

She nodded and looked at Harper. 'I think that will be much more exciting for us all, hey, Harper? Go see the fishes and penguins?'

Being with Harper was exciting—learning about her, becoming a father. But being with Mia was different…more scintillating, more tempting. He needed ordinary—shopping, boring things. Things that wouldn't involve Mia laughing or cooing at penguins, making her more adorable and more appealing.

Sofa shopping…that was where it was at.

But Harper tugged on his hand and her large blue O'Connor eyes tugged at his heart. ''Quarium, Bwin. Fish.'

How could he resist?

'I guess I'm just one big pushover.' He took her chubby little hand in his. 'Okay, come on, princess.'

Mia's hand rested on his back as she chuckled, whispering, 'What is it with daddies and their girls?'

Yeah. His throat tightened. He'd been here before and it had been the best thing that had ever happened in his whole damned life. And this was a great second chance to have it all over again.

A chance and a threat. A huge, scary and dangerous threat.

Pushover—yeah. Been there, done that.

And it had hurt him badly in the end.

He didn't know if he could cope with all of this.

He was a natural, she had to admit.

He listened to Harper's endless chatter, as if she were a wise mentor giving him worldly advice. He laughed at her showing off. He played the blankie game until even Harper got bored of it. Read out all the information posters about each fish and sea creature, pulled faces at the sharks and held Harper when, randomly, she was scared of the penguins. He gave her food before she started to complain about being hungry. Anticipated her toilet needs and gave her space when she needed it, keeping her close in the crowd. His enthusiasm was endless, his patience even more so. It was as if he knew exactly what a good father was and had determined to be exactly that.

And with every smile, cuddle and adoration of Harper, with every side-smile towards her, with every brief accidental touch or brush of fingers…and some not so accidental…she wanted him more.

But something niggled at the back of her mind.

Something that wasn't quite ready to take full form as an idea. Something that wasn't quite right. He was a great parent. Fantastic. He anticipated Harper's needs and knew how to soothe her when she cried. But how? Most people needed time to get used to a child they'd only just met. He wasn't just a 'wee whisperer', he was perfect.

No one was ever perfect.

But he hadn't believed they'd actually turn up today. Why not? Why did he hold some things back? What wasn't he telling her? What had happened to make him so untrusting? She couldn't put her finger on it, but she was going to be more alert to his words and reactions going forward.

By the time they'd got Harper back to the apartment, fed and bathed her, she was exhausted. Mia left Brin reading a bedtime story on the bed with his daughter, snuggled under one of his arms. Unable to hear the soft lilt of his voice without wanting to slide under his other arm and listen to him until she fell asleep too, or at the very least climb right into the bed with him, she wandered into the kitchen, poured herself a wine and sat in the lounge, staring out to sea.

Regardless of her niggling brain, today had gone well. Harper and Brin had a bond, she could see that. She had to make this work.

'She's finally gone to sleep.' His voice jolted her from her daydreams. 'I'm ready to do the same.'

'It was a big day.'

His eyebrows rose. 'For us all.'

'Not one I imagined ever having.'

He'd brought the bottle of wine and another glass through and hovered by the back door. 'Do you want to watch the TV? A film?'

The way he said the word sounded like 'fillum' and it made her chuckle. 'No. I'd like to sit for a while and chill.'

'I have chocolate.' He waved a bar of expensive dark chocolate under her nose.

'Yes please!'

He laughed. 'Come outside and chill, then. Eat chocolate. Watch the sunset. Well, you can't see the actual sunset from here, but the sky is a riot of colour.'

'Chocolate, wine and a beautiful sunset. You know how to treat a girl.'

'My girls.' His gaze latched on to hers and she saw that, regardless of what they'd agreed or how mistrusting he was, he *wanted* this. Wanted her. Which made her heart jitter and her belly squeeze.

There was more to this than a physical attraction. She wanted to know more about him, wanted to understand him. Wanted him with an intensity that took her by surprise.

And it felt so natural to sit next to him on the large wicker sofa, chocolate melting on her tongue, wine in her hand, and look at the beautiful evening sky, which was indeed streaked with vivid oranges and pinks. She gazed up at it and sighed. 'Red sky at night…'

'Shepherd's delight. In Ireland, that means it's going to be a nice day tomorrow. But it means nothing as straightforward here.' He chuckled, his nose crinkling and his eyes glittering. 'New Zealand weather is a mystery to me. One minute it's raining, then it's sunny. Sometimes it's sunny and rainy at the same time. And I've never been anywhere else in the world where you have rain when there's no clouds.'

She nudged him and laughed. 'You'll get used to it. Carry a sunhat and an umbrella wherever you go.'

'Right you are.' He smiled at her. 'I don't suppose you heard anything about Ruth Taylor—the pregnant woman I medevaced last week? How did she get on?'

She didn't want to do small talk. She wanted to curl into his arms, lean her head on his shoulder and watch the colourful clouds scud by. 'Her husband called to let us know she was being kept in hospital to be monitored, but they'd managed to stop the contractions. Baby is happy and snug, Mum's just a bit bored.'

'As you would be for any length of time. It got me thinking, though, about what you went through. I keep trying to imagine you and Harper. Who held her first?'

'Carly. She delivered her, with guidance. She has such love for her niece. That's a bond that will never be broken.'

He blinked, almost as if he was flinching, but recovered. 'Did she cry straight away?'

'Carly? She was sobbing through it all. Worse than me, to be honest.'

He bugged his eyes at her. 'I meant Harper.'

'I know.' She giggled, delighted he wanted to hear so much about it. 'Harper yelled her guts out. She was not entirely happy to be out in the world, despite the hurry.'

'That's my girl—making a big noise.' He winked. 'Stating her place.'

'Oh, she can do that well enough. She doesn't lack confidence. That must come from you.'

He shrugged. 'I hope I'm not too full of myself.'

'Just enough.' Enough confidence, enough sense of humour, enough sex appeal. She looked at the shadows and light in his features. There was so much about him that she liked. But so much about him that she still didn't know. Such as why he'd reacted at the mention of Carly. Or had it been the niece bit?

She slipped her sandals off, twisted to lean against the sofa's arm, popped her feet onto the cushion next to him and looked at him. 'Have you seen many births?'

'More often than not we're getting them to hospital in the nick of time, but I've attended a few. Eleven all up.' He ran his hand over her bare toes, as if they'd spent many evenings like this, chatting about their jobs and lives. Her heart made more space for him. She wiggled her toes and he tickled them, then his palm slid up her calf.

It was difficult to have any kind of proper conversation with his hand on her like this but she persevered. 'Any drama?'

'Actually, no. Just…well, miracles. Special stuff. Magical stuff. It's amazing. All that work and all that worry and then there's this perfect little scrap of life in your hands. Holding your little one when they first breathe or blink… Being the first person they ever see in their whole lives, with those little button eyes… That primeval squawk… Ah.' He looked at her, his eyes bright and soft, and she could see the wonder of it all in his face. Could see the love right there. Then his face fell, and he stopped stroking her leg. 'God, I'm sorry, Mia. I wasn't getting at you.'

Love for who, exactly? Had he been there, feeling that? 'Not at all. I did everything I could to find you, Brin, and I wish you'd been there too. Because you've described exactly how I felt— such joy and worry, this tiny little dot of a thing depending on you, and you love it fiercely, so fiercely, even though it's the first time you've ever met. I get that. I know that, Brin. But there's something else, isn't there? That look in your eye.'

She made her tone gentle and enquiring. He'd actually opened up more in that sentence than she'd ever heard before. 'As if you've been there, holding your baby for the first time.'

He shook his head and looked away. 'Ah, you know. Just what I've seen of other fathers.'

'But it isn't, is it? There's something you're not telling me.' She stroked his shoulder, desperate for him to tell her what had happened.

He blinked and she saw a flicker of panic in his features, which confirmed her suspicions. He blew out a long breath. 'Leave it, Mia. Don't go there. I don't.'

'So there *is* something.'

'Mia.' His tone was a warning. He lifted her feet from his thigh, got up, walked across to the rail and leaned against it, looking out at the sky. Then he turned, his features wrestled into something benign again. 'The problem with my job is that we don't get to hear about many outcomes, so it's nice to find out what's going on with Ruth.'

She held his gaze, waiting for him to rewind back to her questions. She wanted answers. He held her gaze then gave a minute shake of his head, enough to tell her not to intrude any more deeply into his personal life.

Well, something bad had happened, that much she could tell. Was that what had made him leave Ireland? Was that why he was running from job to job and country to country?

And why wouldn't he tell her?

And how would it impact his life going forward?

Because, when it came down to it, they really didn't know each other much at all. Sure, there was an amazing attraction, but heart to hearts, sharing truths and dreams…? Not since that one and only night together.

They were different people now. Getting to know and understand someone took time. Opening themselves up and trusting each other would take even longer. He wasn't going to tell her about his past. Not now, not today. Probably not tomorrow, or next month. Her heart stung at him keeping secrets from her. Their physical distance now felt like an emotional chasm.

But she tried to salvage something of the conversation and followed his lead to not pry. 'Whereas we're there for them before and after. I love the continuity from birth through to old age. No doubt I'll be seeing a lot more of Ruth and her baby when she comes home.'

'You clearly love your job.'

She pulled her feet up and wrapped her arms around her knees. 'I do.'

'And you intend to stay on Rāwhiti?'

'Yes. Why?'

'I wondered if you'd ever thought about moving away?'

Where was this going? 'I spent three years in

the city doing my nursing degree then had various stints in hospitals and clinics across the country, getting more qualified, but no. I don't want to live anywhere else.'

'What about travelling? I remember you said you wanted to explore the world.'

She sighed. 'With a child? That would be difficult.'

'There are ways. You could go and I could look after her.'

'What?' She frowned. He was planning a life without her in it. And, even though she had no right to feel hurt by this, the sting of it rippled through her. 'You're encouraging me to go on holiday and leave her with you?'

'Sure, why not? When she's older, maybe.'

'I can't go away and leave my daughter behind.' A wedge of pain slid into her chest.

He frowned. '*Our* daughter. I'm talking years in the future, Mia. Not tomorrow.'

She'd sold her family home and the guilt and sadness of that rippled through her daily. She was dealing with a flood in her house and her workplace, managing solo parenting and reacquainting with this man who didn't trust her yet. It was a lot.

She was trying to make sense of it all but she felt as if her routine and future were suddenly slipping from under her feet and she was scrambling to stay upright. 'Things are moving too quickly here, Brin. Let's be honest, we need to get to know each other a lot better before we start to make those sorts of plans.' She jumped up and walked to the door.

He followed her. 'Where are you going?'

'To bed. Harper and I have got a lot to do tomorrow.'

'But…'

She put up her hand to silence him. 'It's for the best, I think.'

CHAPTER ELEVEN

A HIGH-PITCHED CRY startled Mia awake. She glanced at the clock: two forty-seven. Her heart raced as she listened again.

Footsteps passed her door.

Harper?

Heart pounding, she jumped out of bed, ran to Harper's room and found Brin about to go in there too. 'What's happening? Is she okay?' he whispered.

Mia put her finger to her lips, aware that she was dressed only in her summer sleepwear comprising a pale blue tank top and barely-there shorts. Aware that his eyes had appraised her as she'd walked towards him.

And that her eyes had appraised his bare chest and dark boxers, toned abdomen and muscled shoulders. Her body thrummed at the sight of his half-naked body. 'Let's take a look.'

They opened the door and peeked in. He was standing behind her and the warmth of his body so close to hers made her breath catch.

Harper was lying on her back, her blankie gripped firmly in one hand, a toy penguin that Brin had bought her from the aquarium in the other.

Mia's heart rippled with love as she edged back out of the room, nudging Brin behind her. 'She's fast asleep. She does that sometimes, just a little cry or a snore. Sleep talking—nothing major.'

'Worth checking, though.'

'Always.'

He started to make his way back down to the lounge but stopped at her…his…bedroom door. 'You okay? You dashed off earlier and you seemed upset.'

Was this really the time for that conversation? But, if not now, when? Over a busy breakfast with Harper? When they were shopping? She wanted Brin to open up with her so she had to talk the talk. 'Oh, you know. I'm confused, to be honest. I'm emotionally all over the place.'

'You too? I was lying there going over and over what we need to do, how to deal with it all. What I'd said that might have upset you. I was an *eejit* to suggest you go on holiday without your daughter. I'm sorry.' His smile almost melted her heart. 'I'm just eager to cram all those missed years into now.'

'Well, I could have dealt with it better. It's wrong of me to be scared you two will develop a bond and freeze me out.' She'd looked deep inside herself and found this ugly jealousy. But she'd had three years carrying and getting to know their daughter—he hadn't. 'I jumped when I should have stayed and talked it through with you. I do want you to spend time with her. Honestly, I do.'

'I wouldn't want someone coming into my life and taking over, taking my daughter away from me. I'm sorry if you thought I was going to do that. Jeez, I would *never* do that. *Ever.* I know what that would do to you.' He looked at her with such conviction that she wondered again: what had happened to him to make him so adamant about this? He breathed out. 'It's early days. We need to take this at your pace, and we've all got to get used to the new status quo. But promise you'll talk to me about how you're feeling. I don't want to break anything you have with Harper, but I do want to grow my own bond with her.'

'I know. I don't want things to change.'

'They will. It's inevitable. But I'll try make it a good change. For us all.'

'Thanks. I know I'll come round to it; just give me time.' He seemed so adamant that he wouldn't take Harper away, she had to believe him.

He clapped his hands. 'Right. I reckon this calls for emergency hot chocolate.'

He walked into the kitchen, switched a light on under one of the cupboards and flicked on the kettle. Mia lifted out cups and put them on the counter. 'That's exactly what my friend Carly would say. She reckons hot chocolate makes everything better.'

He spooned chocolate mix into the cups and turned to look at her. 'She's right about that.'

'And I'm sorry I pried. It's your life. You don't have to tell me everything about your past. But I do want to get to know you better.'

'For Harper or for you?' He stirred water into the cups then carried them through to the lounge and put them on the coffee table.

Good question. She sat next to him on the sofa, picked up her hot chocolate and sipped it. Awareness of his half-naked body fingertips' stretch away thrummed through her body. She wanted to get to know him better in so many ways. And she couldn't keep hiding behind her daughter.

In the dim light his face was shadows. He wouldn't see her reaction. And, if she wanted him to be honest, she had to start too. 'For me, Brin. I want to know you. I feel as if you're giving me only what you want me to see.'

'I'm giving you all I can. I'm sorry if that's not enough. You don't trust me, is that it?'

She stared into her mug. '*I* don't trust *me.*'

'In what way?'

She tried to find words to describe the commotion inside her but came up with nothing that made sense. 'Ignore me. Sorry, it's late, and I'm not making sense. This was probably a mistake.'

'What was?' His fingers found hers and he stroked them. 'Coming here?'

'Yes. And no. You're in our lives now so we have to make something of that. But there's all this attraction getting in the way. I'm scared... angry, confused. And I want to kiss you again. None of it makes sense.'

He smiled wryly. 'No. It doesn't. If it helps, I want to kiss you again too.'

'It doesn't help at all.' Her body rippled with need at his words. She had to stay strong. 'But I'm not the same person I was three years ago. I've spent so long grieving for my family and building a new life for me and Harper. It's taken a lot out of me but I'm stronger for it. I know what I want, who I am.'

'I can see that. You've a lot to be proud of. You've had some terrible things happen in your life and yet you do amazing things, usually with a smile.'

'Apart from when I bit your head off earlier.' She shook her head. Why did he have to be so understanding? 'I hope that one day you'll trust me enough to tell me about what happened to you.'

'Mia...' He shook his head.

Frustration bubbled through her. 'Come on, Brin. I've been completely honest with you about my life. And I think there's things from your past that have impacted us too. That might still do, going forward. And I want to be prepared for that.'

His eyebrows knitted as he picked up his mug and drank. 'Like what?'

'Like, you don't have social media when everyone has *something*. You know a lot about parenting—more than someone like you should. It's not just your job, there's more. You're an uncle, maybe? But why not say something? None of it makes sense. And that first time we met you said you were running. I asked you why and you said, "you don't want to know". Why?'

Putting down his cup, he blew out a breath, opened his mouth, closed it and opened it again. 'Look, it's just demons, nothing dangerous or sinister. Some stuff happened in my past and I want to leave it there.'

'Why?' She knew she was pushing him further than he wanted to go but she wanted to break down this emotional barrier.

'Because what's important is now, Mia. I'm not running any more, that's all you need to know. I'm here. I'll be here for as long as you and Harper need me.'

She drained her cup and put it on the coffee table. 'It's really great for you to say that now, and to promise it too. I believe you mean it. But no one knows what's round the corner. No one can promise "for ever".' Her parents and her brother had thought they'd got many more years with her.

He leant forward, took both of her hands in his and looked deep into her eyes. 'I know you need certainty, Mia. I know you've had a lot of upheaval in your life and I'm not going to add to that, I promise. I want to help. I want to take some of the solo parenting burden from you. I want a relationship with Harper, but not at a cost to you. We can compromise. We can work things out together. Talk things through.'

She could deal with the practicalities. The problem was the threat to her emotional equilibrium. But he was committing to stay, so that was something. He'd also promised not to get in the way of her relationship with her daughter. Maybe she should start believing him.

Here, in the middle of the night, she almost could. Maybe Harper was the thing that had made him stop running—a tether to a new life in a new country. A future he could look forward to instead of looking backwards.

Her heart swelled. If they navigated the right way, they could be good parents together, apart. They could share the load, discuss any issues. She wouldn't be on her own through this. 'Okay.'

And maybe later she'd find out what he'd been running from. He clearly wasn't going to elucidate…he clearly didn't fully trust her.

He dropped her hands and picked up his cup. 'See? I told you hot chocolate was the answer.'

A siren outside had her jumping and looking out of the window. A blur of flashing lights roared along the street below. 'I'm such an island girl, I'm not used to all this city noise.'

'Just the scratching of possums and the call of the *ruru* on Rāwhiti.' He laughed. 'Not sure I could get used to all those eerie animal night-sounds. I like the white noise of the city.'

'*Ruru?*' She sat back and regarded him. 'Owl?'

'Yes. I'm trying to learn a bit of *te reo Māori* so I can help Harper. They teach it in school, don't they?'

'They incorporate some of it into lessons—the basics, like counting—but the general population is far from fluent.'

'Listen...' He held up his hand and counted on his fingers. '*Tahi, rua, toru, whā, rimu, on—*'

'No.' She giggled. '*Rima* is five. *Rimu* is a type of tree.'

He shrugged. 'Ah, you know. It's difficult to learn a language at the ripe old age of thirty-four.'

'Seriously, well done. What else do you know?'

He patted his flat stomach. '*Puku.*'

'Yes, belly.' She laughed, her eyes drawn to muscle that arrowed down below the band of his boxers.

Oh, man. They were half-naked here. She swallowed and forced her gaze back to his face.

His expression had changed. His eyes were still alight with tease and fun but there was something far sexier there too.

'What else?' Her voice sounded breathy, raw and a little high-pitched. She cleared her throat. 'Any more?'

His head moved from side to side in a 'maybe' gesture. 'Okay, but don't laugh.'

'I wouldn't dream of it.'

He chuckled and shook his head. 'You just did.'

'Okay. I promise to *try* not to laugh.' She pressed her lips together and tried to stop smiling but couldn't. His gorgeous Irish accent, fumbling around the unfamiliar *te reo* vowel sounds, was cute as hell. 'Hit me with it.'

He pointed to his eyes. 'Um…*karu.*'

'Yes. Good.' She pointed to her nose. 'This?'

His eyes brightened. 'Yes. I know this one. It's…*ihu.*'

'Very good. And this?' She pointed to her mouth.

He slowly traced his fingertips across her lips. 'I have no idea what the word for lips is.'

She shivered at his touch, her body alight with a sudden intense need for his mouth to be exactly where his fingers were. She wasn't sure she would be able to form any words, but managed, *'Ngutu.'*

His eyes shone with glittering desire. 'You have a beautiful mouth, Mia Edwards.'

'Thank you.' The air around them felt heavy and swollen with need. She tried to breathe, but inhaled stuttering breaths. She touched his mouth with her fingertips. 'You too.'

'The *ting* is…' His voice was so quiet and reverent. 'I can't manage myself around you. You're so damned beautiful, so committed to your daughter and to your friends. You're compassionate and funny.' His thumb ran over her bottom lip. 'And sexy as hell. I can't think straight when I'm with you. All I want to do is…' His words trailed off and he shook his head, moving away his hand.

She couldn't bear *not* to be touched. 'What? What do you want to do?'

'All I want to do is kiss you, Mia. That night we shared has been going over and over in my head for the last three years—taunting me, haunting me, exciting me. I've said it before—it was magical. Like a dream.'

Fire rolled through her, razing any rational thought. Every cell in her body craved his touch. Earlier she'd thought things were moving too quickly but now things were not moving quickly enough. She desperately wanted to hold him, to feel his strength around her. To sink into what they were both afraid of: that connection and intimacy. The attraction growing between them that was undeniable and off the scale.

Hell, if she didn't touch him, she didn't know what she'd do. 'It was real, Brin. Like this is very, very real.'

'But what the hell are we going to do about it?' He shook his head and laughed, as if it was all so hopeless, but she caught hold of his hand. 'We know it's reckless to give in to it. We can't.'

Reckless? Yes. She wanted to be exactly that. It had been so long since she'd let go of control on her emotions, her life and her heart. When her family had died she'd held on. When she'd discovered she was pregnant to a man she couldn't find again, she'd held on. She'd had to because she'd had no one to catch her if she'd let go. It had been years since she'd been touched, held, loved, caught.

Three years, to be exact. No man had ever instilled in her such need. No man had so much as captured her interest, never mind her heart. Not like Brin. He captured her thoughts, her heart and her soul. And she needed more from him. More scorching kisses, yes. More touching. Sitting here and not touching him, seeing him half-naked, being with him, made her feel dizzy with need.

If he was too good a man to initiate anything, then she would take control.

'Touch me.' She placed his palm on her chest. 'Here.'

'Mia.' His eyes widened as he groaned, a warning and a desperate prayer of reverence.

'Feel my heart. It's beating so fast because I want you so much. I want you to touch me.' Then she slid his hand down to her breast. 'Here.'

His eyes shuttered closed briefly, as if he was trying to stay in control but rapidly losing his grasp. He opened them again and ran his fingers over her nipple. There was no bra, just her thin tank top, and her nipples reacted immediately to his touch. '*God*, Brin. That's good.'

'Jeez, Mia. You're killing me.' He looked as if he wanted to devour her.

She held out her wrist to his face, the spot where she'd sprayed her perfume this morning, wondering who she was applying it for. Why she was putting on perfume, make-up, choosing her favourite clothes and packing skimpy nightwear.

It was all for him. 'Breathe me in.'

He did as she said and he smiled, pulling her across the sofa and nuzzling her neck. 'I love the way you smell—flowers and something that's just you. It's addictive.'

She curled into his touch, putting her hand where his warm breath grazed her skin. Desire wound through her like a fire. She pressed her cheek against his, breathing in his scent. 'You smell exactly as I remember, Brin. It's so damned hot. I can't resist.'

'It's the hot chocolate. Magic.' He chuckled as his hands skimmed down her sides, grazing the side of her breasts on the way to her hips, and he held her there in place.

'It's not that.' She smiled as she caught his gaze. 'It's everything about you, Brin, driving me wild.'

'I think I'd like it when you're wild.' He angled

his head and for a moment she thought he might kiss her, but she wanted to keep her flimsy grip on control for one moment longer, so she moved back a few inches.

'See me.' She slipped off her top, revealing her naked breasts. She felt reckless, sexy, fun, desired…wanted.

He gasped and ran his fingertips over her beaded nipple. 'I have no words, Mia. You are even more beautiful than I remember.'

'I doubt that. I have stretch marks and I'm not as toned as I was.' The first time with him, she'd had nothing to lose. It had been a one-night thing and she'd thought she'd never see him again. Yet here he was, inextricably linked to her for ever. This time, her heart and her life were on the line. But not even that thought could douse the flames of desire inside her.

'You've done the most amazing thing, Mia.' His fingers trailed over her skin. His eyes gazed down at her, hot and intense. 'This body has grown and nursed a child. Our child. It's a work of bloody art.'

Her thoughts blurred as he stroked her breast. All she wanted, all she could think of, was to kiss him, taste him and feel him rock deep inside her. This man who had stalked her dreams for too long. He was here. He was real and he was hers. More, he was better than she remembered—kinder, funnier, sexier. He made her feel cared for and beautiful. Quite simply, he made her feel happy.

She shuddered, finally losing her grip on control. She crawled onto his lap and felt the hard rock of his erection underneath her core as she straddled him. 'Taste me.'

CHAPTER TWELVE

BRIN GROANED AS her lips touched his. All his attempts at denying their chemistry were faded memories. All sensible thoughts had vacated his brain. Because this could not, should not, be denied. He wrapped his arms around her waist and hauled her close.

He let her take the lead with sweet, soft kisses until he couldn't hold back any longer. He kissed her, hard and deep, cupping her breast, feeling the delicious swell of her in his palm, the tight nub under his fingertips. Then he slicked kisses down her throat to her breast. He sucked in her nipple and she bucked against him, writhing on his erection.

Her movements were rhythmical, incredible and so damned sexy, and he was fighting to hold on. He flipped her onto her back and slipped off her sleep shorts.

Then he kissed across her breast until he reached her nipple again. He sucked it in and felt the shiver of need ripple through her, the contraction of her belly. Her hands slid into his hair and she moaned as he kissed a trail lower, across the flat ridges of her rib cage to the soft sweep of her hip.

He paused as he looked more closely at the silvery lines below her belly button—the map of motherhood.

His throat suddenly raw, he traced the lines and wondered how she'd looked when ripe with his child.

'Brin!' She gasped, her hand on his cheek. 'I'm so sorry you weren't there. It was a miracle. She is our little miracle.'

'You are the miracle, Mia.' He kissed the silvery skin then dipped his head lower to the crest between her thighs. He parted her legs and stroked her centre. Slipped one finger then another into her silky softness.

She let go of his hair and lay back, moaning and whimpering with pleasure as he replaced his fingers with his mouth.

'Brin. Brin. Oh…' She rocked her hips against his mouth and he held her hips tight as she rode her pleasure. Her back arched as her body tensed and he tasted her sweet hotness. 'I need you inside me, Brin.'

'No way. Not yet.' He matched her frantic rhythm and felt the tightness swell around his fingers as she called his name.

'Now, Brin. Please. Now.'

The desperation in her voice matched the feeling in his skin, in his gut and lower, deeper. Urgency and need were stoked by her pleasure. He climbed back up the length of her, skin against skin.

Breast. Throat. Mouth. Lips. Hot. Wet.

'Up,' she commanded, encouraging him to lift his backside off the couch. She slid off his boxers and took him in her hand.

Her palm on his erection sent sparks of heat shimmering through him. He laughed, groaned and sighed at the same time. 'You're in one hell of a hurry.'

'It's been three years.' She laughed.

'It'll be over in three seconds if you don't stop.'

Condom...

'Condom.'

Wallet. Jeans. Floor. He reached, grabbed and tore then was sheathed, her mouth a constant on his neck, his cheek, his mouth.

He positioned himself between her legs and she clutched at his skin, urging him on. He kissed her again then, capturing her in a wet, open-mouthed, messy kiss. Then he gently nudged inside her. Her heat subsumed him and it took all his strength to hold back. He paused as she inhaled sharply. 'You okay, Mia?'

'Yes. Yes.'

'I can't believe this is happening.'

She held his face in her hands. 'I never forgot you, Brin. Not ever. I wanted you so much, through it all. I looked for you.'

'You found me.' He kissed her mouth, the bridge of her nose, her cheeks. 'I'm here, Mia. Here for you.'

'Those damned Fates meddling again.' Her eyes filled with tears but she blinked them away.

'Thank goodness.' He brushed her hair back, capturing her gaze, staring at those sultry brown eyes that had bewitched him from the start. At the mouth that had entranced him, mesmerised him. This fierce, soft, serious, funny, sexy woman had blown his mind and filled his chest with heat.

He pushed a little deeper inside her then pulled out.

'More,' she cried against his collarbone, bucking against him.

He caught her rhythm in long, deep strokes, felt white heat. With each stroke, pleasure balled inside him, tighter and tighter. She grabbed at his shoulders and he pulled her closer to get deeper, clawing, reaching, kissing until there was no air or space between them.

He felt her tighten around him, her head lolling back as she shuddered. 'Come with me, Brin.'

The way she said his name, like a solemn oath, was his undoing. He closed his eyes, rocked deeper and harder and chased her release over the edge until he was flying and falling.

Falling hard for the woman who had fallen into him three years ago.

After, once his heart had stopped ramming against his rib cage and he could breathe again, he tucked her into the crook of his arm and kissed the top of her head, breathing in the scent he'd craved for so long. He remembered how incredible it had felt last time, and this time had been five times more intense. He nuzzled her hair. 'That was amazing.'

'More than amazing.' Her laughter was light and a balm to his soul. She snuggled against him, branding him with her scent. Which was unnecessary: he was hers now anyway. And, truthfully, he'd been hers for the last three years. 'No tears this time. Well, almost, but I held it together.'

He squeezed her shoulder, remembering the way she'd sobbed that night in the hotel and how he'd cradled her. How this time was different—deeper, better.

He felt her cheek move against his chest and knew she was smiling. 'Is holding it together such a good thing?'

'I don't want to be that sobbing, emotional wreck I was back then.'

'Why not?' He edged back, creating space to look at her. 'Just be you, Mia.'

She sat up and looked at him, stroking her fingers down his cheek. 'I told you, I've changed. I'm older and wiser.'

'Or maybe you hide the pain of losing your family better. But I see it sometimes, in the way you stare out at the sea; the little frown at the storm clouds, as if you're telling them to back off. Sometimes it's an expression you have: I know you're thinking of them. I wish I could do something to make it better.'

Her eyes misted. 'It won't ever be better. I've just learnt to live with it. They're gone. They're never coming back.'

He took her hand and stroked little circles over her palm with his thumb. 'It takes time to come to that conclusion, right? You grieve, you hope, you get angry. You scream. And then eventually you realise that, no matter what you want, it's never going to happen.'

She stared at him for a few moments, as if trying to work out something, then asked, 'Who have you lost, Brin?'

Oh, damn.

There he was again, his mouth running away with itself, his brain hurrying to catch up too late. He scrambled for a palatable answer that wasn't lies, exactly, and might be enough to assuage her curiosity. 'Just…er…my dad.'

'Oh? All that emotion for losing someone you didn't like.' She frowned, her gaze intensifying.

'It doesn't ring true, Brin. Losing your mum, yes. But your dad? I think that's just a facade.'

Why hadn't he said his mum?

Her eyes narrowed. 'You also once said that a woman lied to you and that was why you didn't like me lying about my name. What happened, Brin? I need to know how to put all the jigsaw pieces together.'

Hurt pricked him. He'd thought he'd dealt with it, but he was reminded that nothing lasted for ever, even times like this with a beautiful woman and a warm heart. 'Some things are best not being known, Mia.'

'Bull.' She scrambled back up the bed and frowned, bunching the duvet round her naked body like a shield. 'You're deliberately being obtuse. How can we forge a relationship of any kind if you allude but don't explain? I'm not a mind reader, but if this affects us then I need to know.'

'It won't affect us.'

She pointed to the space between them. 'It already has.'

His gut tightened. Mia was right. She was pretty much always right. His obfuscation had only led to more questions. Avoidance wasn't working. If he didn't let go of the ache of his past, he might not wholly be able to move forward.

The weight of it all pressed on his chest, the past and the present—the little girl he'd lost and the one he'd just found. The betrayal of trust that had him running, and this new feeling with Mia that he wanted to sink into. But he'd been mired in his negativity for so long, he wasn't sure how to unstick himself.

'Jeez, Mia. To be honest, I don't even know where to start. And if I do start, I don't know…' He ran his hand over his hair. Was bringing this negativity into their space wise?

Her tone was gentle. She covered his hand with hers. 'Don't know what?'

'If I'll be able to stop.'

She smiled softly and encouragingly. 'Oh, I know how that feels. It builds up inside, right? You want to throw things. Sometimes you don't think you can bear the pain any longer—you wish you felt numb. But feeling nothing is scary. I get it. I don't know what you've been through, but I get it.'

He breathed out. This amazing woman had been through so much, had lost so much, yet here she was, understanding him. Getting him. How could his pain ever match hers?

He owed her so much, owed himself so much, to give voice to what had been haunting him. And hopefully, by doing that, he'd let it go. 'I was married, Mia.'

Her eyes widened, and she looked briefly wrong-footed, but she nodded, digesting it all. 'Sure, you're thirty-four. We've all got baggage.'

'It wasn't the plan. The wedding, the baby—

they were road bumps. We were just out of college and had secured jobs on a cruise ship. We were going to travel the world, but she fell pregnant, so we gave up those dreams and built a different life. We did the whole grown-up package: house, jobs, baby. We had a beautiful girl, Niamh. I watched her mother give birth to her. Celebrated her first steps, first words, first day at school. It was everything. We tried to make it work. I was happy.'

'And what happened?' Mia's eyes had filled with tears and her hand was at her mouth. 'Oh, Brin…she didn't…did she…?'

But he shook his head quickly. 'It's not what you think. She wasn't hurt. She didn't die. She's fine. She's okay. She's healthy, she's good. I think.'

Mia breathed out. 'You *think*? You've got another daughter who you *think* is okay?'

He imagined what might be going through her head. 'I didn't abandon her. I would never do that. I loved her. *Love* her.'

'So…what happened? Why don't you know she's okay? Why isn't she here with you?'

He knew Mia couldn't contemplate being separated from her daughter even for one minute, never mind years. 'One day I came home early from work and found my wife in bed with my brother. As I confronted them, he proudly announced he was Niamh's father. That they'd been having an on-off kind of thing for years.'

'Oh, Brin. I'm so sorry. And she knew he was the father?'

'Yes. But she hadn't dared tell me. I guess she thought she'd pick the most reliable brother to bring up her child. The one who'd stick with her. When I caught them, she'd only just confessed the truth to him. A later DNA test proved it.'

Rage rippled through him even now. His brother—the one person he'd trusted more than anyone else in his life. They'd been inseparable growing up. United against a father who'd deserted them. United in their love for their mother. They'd shared the same blood, the same house, the same upbringing. But that was where the similarities ended. DNA could only connect them so far.

And his wife—the other person he'd loved, respected and trusted. How? Why? Why had they done that to him? It was so beyond his own standards and morals, he still couldn't fathom it.

But Mia's hand on his back soothed some of it as she said, 'I can't imagine how you felt, Brin. To have that kind of betrayal after giving up everything for them. After believing she was your girl. It must have hurt you so much.'

'I was stunned. I'd had no idea. I thought we were both happy.' There'd been no signs...or maybe there had been but he'd been delusional.

Had allowed himself to sink into a dream. He wasn't going to let that happen again.

'Your brother, too. That's awful.'

'You should have seen him, Mia. He was hateful. Spiteful. Gunning for a fight. I don't know what I'd done for him to be like that.'

'Jealousy, maybe? You married "his" woman.'

'Grainne was my girlfriend. My wife. But maybe he hated that I was happy with her. That we had this family. *Family!*' He snorted. 'The only good thing was that I was the one who'd been at Niamh's birth, not him. I changed her nappies, I saw her grow every single day, not him. He missed out on all those milestones.'

'And now? They're still together?'

'No.' He didn't know whether he was glad about this or just sad at the whole sorry outcome. 'They broke up soon after the truth got out. Turns out neither of us O'Connor boys could trust her. But he gets to see Niamh, not me.'

'But why can't you see her? She's still your niece.'

'Yes. And I love her still. Do you think I'd give up that easily?' He knew his tone had been sharp. 'Sorry. I shouldn't have barked at you.'

But she gave him a soft smile. 'It's only natural to be upset about this. I know you, Brin. You would have fought for her.'

'I insisted I had access. I made her promise I could see Niamh at weekends, evenings. But they moved away to another town for a fresh start.' He shook his head. 'Because everyone we knew had found out and she couldn't cope with the backlash. But, once she'd gone, she made contact very difficult. Wouldn't answer my calls, turned up late for my afternoons with my girl. She told Niamh things about me that weren't true, which Niamh believed. She was…what?…nine or ten at this point. She was encouraged to call my brother, Padraig, "Daddy". Grainne said it was all too confusing for her to have me there too. I was…'

He breathed out his anger. 'The guy who'd brought her up for a few years. I tried, you know? I tried so hard to be the best kind of father. I was involved, interested, invested. It wasn't her fault her parents were messed up. She deserved to have me in her life. A steadiness. I'd been there all along. But then…'

'Then what?'

'Then Niamh announced she didn't want to see me. Parroted reasons from her mother. And I didn't have any options. I wasn't going to make her feel bad or cause trouble. I had no hold over any of them. She isn't my child, however much I want it to be so. I was just…paying.' Paying not only with money but with his trust too. 'Easily discarded as soon as the truth came out.'

'Oh, Brin.' Mia ran her hand down his back then sucked in a sharp breath. 'Now I understand why you needed the test, why you don't trust me to turn up. I would never do those things to you.'

'I know you wouldn't…' He paused because there were still traces of doubt at the back of his mind—not because of Mia, but because of Grainne.

Mia stilled, her eyes narrowing. 'But…?'

He raked his hand across his jaw. 'It's so much, you and me. It's like a flashpoint of need. But what happens when that flashpoint dims? Or stops altogether? I'm struggling with all this, Mia. What if something happened between us and that made you stop me seeing Harper? I've got no power here. You could do the same thing to me and then where would I be?'

Her eyes flashed bright steel. 'I am not your ex.'

'I know. You are far, far from that.' He reached out and stroked her cheek. 'Not in the same universe.'

She smiled. 'I would hope not. And see? Talking about it has made things clearer, helped me understand you a little more—why you were so adamant about the DNA test. Why you were angry about me giving you a false name. Even though I had good reasons, I can see why you'd be unwilling to believe anything I said. I wish you'd told me before.'

'How? When? We're just beginning here, Mia.

This is the kind of thing you talk about when you trust someone. Not before.'

Her eyes widened, her smile reaching them and glittering there in the deep pools of brown. 'You trust me?'

Did he? His chest felt blown open. His pain eased. Hope shimmered, almost in reach, because he thought he actually might. 'Enough that I know you're not like Grainne. And I don't talk about it because I want to forget what happened, you know? Not forget Niamh—never—but I want to cut ties with my brother and with Grainne. I don't do the social media thing because I don't want to read about how they're doing, who they're with, what they had for breakfast. I don't care. I don't care about them at all.' He blew out a breath. 'And now you know everything about me.'

Except she didn't know about the panic rattling through his chest. The raw need for her. Even he didn't understand why it was so intense. Why the flashpoints of need hadn't dimmed.

Yet.

Because they inevitably would. Love didn't last. It was all tied up in pretence. His failed marriage and his brother's betrayal had taught him that.

But she might have suspected what he needed, because she edged closer and wrapped her arms round his neck. 'You're a good man, Brin O'Connor. You didn't deserve any of that. You lived through hell, had your precious daughter taken away. And now here you are, facing it all again. Facing it with dignity and hope. I wouldn't do that to you. Harper is one hundred percent your daughter.'

If he was honest, he didn't dare to hope. He was living day to day here, minute to minute.

Feeling her skin against his had all thoughts of his past evaporating. She pressed her mouth to his and kissed him, long and slow, until his heart didn't ache for what had happened: it sprang to life with the now. He wanted this, he wanted her. Now.

He'd deal with what the future held later.

CHAPTER THIRTEEN

MIA MADE SURE she was early meeting Brin from the ferry—no toilet stops to make him think they weren't going to be there.

It was his third visit in four weeks, a routine of sorts. The start of something, maybe. Each time he visited, they ended up in bed. There was no way of controlling their desire, so they'd agreed to go with it.

Each visit, he helped with fixing up the house—a coat of paint, putting together flat-pack furniture, tiling the kitchen, building a home for Mia and Harper to live in.

But not for Brin to live in. Because that had not been discussed. Neither had they made the step to suggest Harper call him 'Daddy'. But it was coming; they both knew it. Harper was more and more entranced by him every day and the feeling was clearly mutual.

Brin kept pushing for them to tell Harper he was her father…whatever that would mean to a two-year-old. Truth was, Mia wouldn't be able to bear it if Harper lost her father, like Mia had lost hers. She couldn't bear to think of her daughter suffering such a loss, so she held off.

So, what *this* was, she didn't know. They hadn't put a label on it.

It had been wonderful for him to confide in her at last. But, regardless of what he said about his brother, he did care. Mia could see that. He'd been hurt very badly and was trying to be a good man and a good father to Harper, and she'd pushed him to talk, assuming he was hiding something that might damage Harper or her. The truth was, it was something that had damaged him. The hurt in his eyes told her he was still struggling at the loss of his first daughter.

Her heart jumped as he strolled off the ferry, his holdall slung over his shoulder, his eyes bright and smile wide.

God, she'd missed him.

He wrapped her into his arms and kissed her. And she didn't much care about people seeing her like this. Regardless of what he thought, he did have power in this. Power to make her breathless with a touch. Power to make her cry out his name. Power to make her dizzy with need. But in the matter of their daughter, yes, the law would doubtless be on her side. That was why he hadn't trusted they'd turn up and had almost left them standing on the dock. His trust in people had been trashed.

'Where's Harper?' He drew away but kept an arm round her waist as they walked along the harbour front.

'She's at a birthday party.' She shot him a smile. 'So, we get to play.'

He grinned, his eyes twinkling with promise. 'I like the sound of that.'

'With a new flat-pack set of drawers for Harper's room.'

'Oh, you know how to talk dirty. I can't wait to get my hands on that. And you.' He pulled her in for another kiss. 'One set of drawers, then I get to lose myself in you. Deal?'

'Deal.' If she could wait that long. 'I've got some lovely *Frozen* decals to stick on it. I want it to be a surprise when she comes home.'

'Sounds perfect.' He slid his hand into hers. 'Missed me?'

'Only your screwdriver.'

'More dirty talk.' He winked. 'Lead on.'

The buzz of a drill coming from inside her house had her pausing, her hand on Brin's chest. 'Oh, yes, forgot to say, Nikau's finishing off wiring in the new lights in the lounge.'

His eyebrows knitted. 'I could have done that.'

'Nikau's the island's handyman. I willingly pay him. If you or I did that kind of thing, he'd be out of a job.' She leaned against him. 'Besides, I have other ideas for you.'

He nuzzled in her hair. 'Can't wait—'

A loud bang and weird fizzing noise cut him off.

'What the hell?' Mia ran towards the sound that had come from inside her house. Nikau was sprawled on the lounge floor with a cable still in his hand, shattered glass and ceiling plaster around him and an upended stepladder near his feet.

'Stop!' Brin was at her heels. 'He's been shocked. Don't touch him.'

'I've got it.' Heart pounding, she ran to the electrical switch box in the kitchen and flicked it off. 'Okay. The electricity's off now.'

Brin nodded and bent to examine her friend, feeling for a pulse and checking his breathing. 'His pulse is rapid and weak. He also could have hit his head or hurt his back when he fell. Nikau? Nikau, can you hear me?'

The slightest of head movements, a flicker of eyelids.

Mia breathed out. He was alive; that was something. 'I'll get the portable ECG and Owen. And call for an evacuation.'

Brin gave her a sharp nod of approval. 'And adenosine, if you've got it. Just in case.'

When she returned, she found Brin assessing a nasty electrical burn on Nikau's palm. She knelt down next to him. 'Here's some saline solution and an IV set. Owen's out on a call but Anahera's coming over. Chopper's on its way.'

Brin smiled and took the ECG from her. 'Thanks. You're good at this.'

'It's what I do.' These were her friends. More... they were her *whanau*, her family, and she'd move heaven and earth for them. She shrugged but felt pride shimmer through her. 'Right, Nikau, bear with me while I put up a drip with some fluids for you.'

'Have you got any pain in your back? Neck? Legs?' Brin did a thorough assessment and Mia was mightily relieved when she saw their patient move his arms and legs. Even so, she applied a neck brace and kept him still while Brin completed his examination.

Anahera came running through the door and threw herself at her son on the floor. 'Nikau. Oh God, Nikau.'

'Be careful of the broken glass,' Mia said, shifting sideways to let Anahera closer to her son.

Nikau blinked at the sound of his mother's wails. He raised a hand. 'I'm...okay...'

'We've called for an evac.' Brin looked from mother to son. 'He's had a nasty electric shock and some burning on his hand. We need to monitor his heart rate and make sure he didn't damage his neck or back when he fell from the stepladder.'

'Aren't I always telling you to be careful?' Anahera shook her head and stroked the back of Nikau's good hand. 'Thirty-five and still my baby.' She turned to Mia. 'You never have a decent sleep again, once you have kids. Even when they've left home. You always worry.'

'Too right.' Brin shot a sideways look at Mia and winked. His smile was tender, a secret shared.

Mia nodded. 'I don't think I've slept properly since Harper was born.'

Brin's smile slid and he looked...sad. He'd missed out on Harper. How hard must it have been for him to have no contact with Niamh too? How much must he have worried about her? He wouldn't be able to switch off that kind of parental love. No wonder he'd been running for the last few years, essentially trying to come to terms with losing a child. Never mind the break-up of his marriage and the bomb that his brother had detonated in his family.

She realised Anahera was looking at them both, confusion and questions in her expression. Mia had never discussed her private life with anyone here on the island. But she'd kissed Brin in broad daylight now so many times, she had no doubt the gossip machine was in full swing. She wasn't sure how she felt about that.

No one knew Brin was Harper's father, but was it only a matter of time before she let that slip into conversation too? Was she letting things get too cosy, being lured into a false sense of happy families? Was not putting a label on their relationship going to be a recipe for disaster? Did she and Brin have different slants on the way things were developing between them?

'Mumma! Mumma! I got a ice block!' Harper ran through the door with Carly and Mason in quick pursuit. They all stopped at the sight of the little huddle around Nikau on the floor.

Carly took in the scene and quickly moved the children behind her so they couldn't see the unfolding drama. 'Need a hand?'

'All okay, thanks.' Brin nodded. 'Helicopter's on its way.'

'Got you. Okay, kids, it looks like Mummy's busy. Let's go sit outside and eat the ice blocks.' Carly waved. 'In fact, we could have Harper stay the night?'

Brin and Mia both looked at each other.

They could have a child-free night, knowing that Harper would be safe at her auntie's house. They could talk freely about where things were going.

'Yes,' Mia said.

'No,' Brin said at the same time.

She flicked him a confused frown as something akin to rejection skittered through her gut. Did he not want to spend the night with her?

'I thought you needed me to do some DIY?' He bugged his eyes at her. 'For Harper?'

Ah, that. He wanted to see Harper's surprise. 'Yes, of course.'

'Then we can have dinner together.' He grinned. 'The three of us.'

Mia checked herself because, after what he'd been through, he deserved to spend as much time with Harper as he could. She nodded at Carly. 'Okay. I'll come and pick her up in…?'

She looked at Brin for an answer. Since when had she deferred to someone else over decisions about Harper?

'Two hours?' Brin nodded at Mia.

'Okay. Shout if you need anything.' Carly gave them a thumbs-up sign. 'See you later.'

Anahera glanced at them both again and smiled knowingly. Then the sound of a helicopter rent the air and Mia focused back on their patient.

Thirty minutes later she was back in her house with Brin at her side, clearing up the glass and ceiling plaster. 'Thank goodness we arrived when we did. Thanks for helping out there.'

'Hey, it's my job.' Brin grinned. 'But, is it my imagination, or is there always a drama when I'm here?'

'Aw, no. Rāwhiti is a peaceful little idyll.'

'Except for cyclones and storms and electrical incidents and early labours…'

'That's what makes it special. Come, look outside.' She took his hand and drew him to the window. 'Look at that perfect blue sky, the little boats bobbing on the ocean. The bush across the bay. It's sublime.'

As she pointed, she glanced up at his face. Oh, he was smiling and nodding, but it was clear he wasn't as enamoured as she was. He didn't want to live here. This place wasn't imprinted in his DNA as it was hers. He didn't see the beauty, the community. Sure, he helped them; he was a good man. But he came here to see his daughter and to see Mia and she knew, without a shadow of a doubt, that he'd have gone anywhere they were. Rāwhiti was just another place to him, not a special one. He didn't have the history and the memories here.

So they needed to make some.

And here she'd been, lulling herself into thinking there might be a future as she peered across the water that had taken her family.

But Brin whirled round to face her and skimmed his hands round her waist, tugging her to him. 'It's pretty and all that, but I prefer this view. Very much.'

She placed her palm on his cheek and traced her thumb across his lips, wanting to erase all thought of her family's tragic end and fill her head with him. 'Well, I guess you're not onerous to look at either.'

His eyes danced with tease as he leaned closer

and whispered, 'You are one hell of a woman, Mia Edwards. Come here.'

He slid his mouth over hers, kissing her long and slow. She wound her arms round his neck and sank into it all—to him, the kiss, the feel of him. And, as always, like a spark to a flame, one touch of his lips on hers made her body come alive with need.

What started as a tender kiss became frantic and desperate. Without lifting his mouth from hers, he slid down the straps of her dress. It pooled around her feet. She stepped out and tugged at his T-shirt, ripping it from his shorts' waistband and pulling it over his head, then making quick work of his shorts.

He laughed. 'What's the hurry? We've got plenty of time before we pick Harper up.'

'I need you, Brin. Inside me. I can't explain. I...'

'I know. I know.' He took both her hands and kissed them. 'You're like a drug. I can't get enough. All I could think of was getting here. The hours at work went so slowly. I love my job, but man, I needed to see you. I needed to do this. I need you.'

He slipped his hands behind her back and unclipped her bra. Then he stepped back to look at her. The intensity of his gaze heated every part of her. Her longing for him grew deeper and deeper every day through their messages and conversations, through the flowers he sent and the presents he brought over for Harper.

I need you.

She tried to be guarded around him, to hold back the truth of her feelings, but it was getting harder to deny them. And to deny all the complications that all this created.

But, oh, the way he caressed her, and the sweet roughness of his kisses, flared her need. She pulled him to her bedroom and removed the last of their underwear before they tumbled onto the bed.

Then he was sheathed and inside her. She held him tight, gripping his shoulders, wrapping her legs round his hips. Wanting to be over him, on him, next to him. Just him—Brin. Always Brin.

Every time she saw him was like the first time. It was filled with wonder, excitement and a building pressure of need in her skin, in her belly. She couldn't think straight until she'd kissed him or made love with him. Until the first rush of desire had been sated. Until the next built, rapidly, and burned through her.

This time it was slow and intense. He held her gaze as he entered her and with each stroke. He watched her as he kissed her, his eyes on hers. A meeting of need and more—so much more. A knowing, an understanding—deep. Soul-deep.

Then suddenly it was too slow and she bucked her hips, changing the angle so he could go deeper and harder. As he slid into her, she felt a growing light there. She chased it with her rhythm, over and over, higher and higher. 'Brin. I can't… Don't stop. Don't stop.'

'This is so good. We're so good together.' His blue eyes were swirling with affection, bright with light.

'Yes.' She urged him to rock faster as need spiralled. 'Yes.'

'You are so damned sexy.' He pushed harder into her, grinding his hips against hers until his body arched and he groaned her name. He was chasing the same light, chasing the release. She gripped his shoulders as it finally crashed through her.

He hauled her close, tight against him, as he pulsed inside her. 'Mia. Jeez. This…is everything.'

Everything.

Yes. Everything she ever wanted was right here.

She giggled as she loosened her grip on his shoulders. 'Happy now?'

'Very happy.' He pressed his forehead to hers as his breathing normalised. 'But I could be happier again in…say…ten minutes? Give me a chance to get my strength back.'

'So soon?' She laughed but had to admit a rerun would be very nice indeed. 'You are incorrigible.'

He shrugged and smiled. 'And insatiable when it comes to you.'

His fingertips ran little circles between her breasts, and he looked at her, smiling lazily. In that smile was a riot of emotions: tenderness; generosity; safety; vulnerability; strength.

In essence, it was Brin O'Connor stripped bare of any pretence, any guard, any mistrust. A naked honesty. This thing between them was as true and raw for him, as it was for her.

As he gazed at her, her heart felt as if it was filled with light. Her whole body cleaved to him. She felt excited and sated. Calm and yet vibrant. The minute she looked at him, this sense of something special filled her. It was the most intense, the most beautiful, feeling she'd ever had.

What was it about him? What was this feeling, that she couldn't bear to be apart from him? That she thought about him every moment of her waking life and many of her sleeping ones too? That her heart beat a special way when she saw him, that her soul felt lighter when she was with him? That he was her person. Her *one*. A final piece in her jigsaw puzzle.

Brin O'Connor.

Then it dawned on her, a slow realisation that stole through her unasked for, unwanted, unbidden: she'd fallen deeper than she'd ever thought possible. She cared for him. She wanted to make him happy, to ease his hurt. She wanted to wake up with him tomorrow and the next day and the next. She'd been fooling herself that she'd met him early at the ferry to ease his mind: it had been because she couldn't wait to see him. To kiss him. To spend their precious moments together. She ached for him.

She was falling in love with him.

Had fallen. Hard and deep.

And that only meant one thing: now…now she was at risk of losing him. Somehow, some time, somewhere. She'd believe he would always be here for her, with her. And one day he wouldn't come back.

And this time she didn't know how she'd survive.

Panic ripped through her. She eased away.

She couldn't love him.

They lived too far apart. It was too soon. It was folly.

It was danger.

CHAPTER FOURTEEN

BRIN WAS TRYING to make sense of the flat-pack instructions when Mia stuck her nose round the door. Her hair was mussed and she had sleep lines down one side of her face. In a nutshell: gorgeous. She yawned. 'Sorry, I must have dozed off.'

'You looked so peaceful, I didn't want to wake you.'

'I didn't realise I was so tired.' She came and sat on the floor next to him, close but with no kiss, no touch. She was probably reeling from her afternoon nap. She'd dressed again, not in her summer dress but in jeans and a long-sleeve top, as if she was cold despite the thirty-degrees day. 'You've been busy.'

He screwed in the last screw and moved back to admire his handiwork. 'I wanted to get this fixed up for when Harper gets home. I can't wait to see her face when she sees it.'

'She'll love it. She's impressed with everything you do. She's always talking about Brin this, Brin that.'

'Brin. I don't want that any more. When do we explain that I'm her daddy?' The words slipped out too quickly. He'd been thinking about bringing the subject up again but hadn't planned what he was going to say. Being here, surrounded by his daughter's things, had him wishing.

Mia's eyes briefly flickered closed and she looked as if she was trying to find the right words, to let him down gently. 'In time, Brin.'

'When?' It was always 'in time', 'it's too early'. He tried to control his irritation as he applied the *Frozen* decals to the drawers.

She blew out a breath. 'Look, I don't know. I don't know how to say it: "Harper... Brin is your daddy". I mean, she understands that Owen is Mason's daddy, and that other kids have daddies, but will she be confused?'

'We could just say it. See how it resonates.' He wanted that. He also knew that he shouldn't push things. Mia was still getting used to having him in her life. Harper was still getting to know him. He wanted too much.

He wanted to lie with Mia until the sun rose. Until they were awakened by their daughter running into their bedroom. Until...

Until what, exactly? In Brin's experience 'for ever' was a distant dream that happened to other people. Or was cruelly snatched away by lies.

His brother had a lot to answer for. Because stealing his family hadn't been enough, no—he'd planted the seeds of mistrust into Brin's head and he'd let them grow.

But he had to keep showing up for his daughter. And he would. 'I'm here, Mia. I'm not going anywhere. The sooner we say it, the better. Then we can all get used to it.'

'It's a big step.' Mia sighed again and wrung her hands. There was something about her demeanour that wasn't quite right. Last week she would have sat on his knee, swiped a kiss on his head. Maybe she was still sleepy, but did he detect some emotional distance too? Was the smile not as ready? Was there some fragility in her voice?

Maybe she didn't believe in 'for ever' either. His heart crumpled. 'But it's the truth. Maybe we should have done it from the beginning.'

She looked at him for a long time and said nothing. A host of different emotions flickered across her features: confusion, worry and then something else. Something he didn't want to put a name to but he felt like a swift blow to his chest.

Eventually, she nodded. 'Okay. We can talk to her when I bring her back from Carly's. In fact, I should head over there now. We said two hours and it's been closer to three.'

'Okay.' Despite the fleeting wariness in her demeanour, his chest heated at the thought of the three of them being together again. 'I'll move the furniture around so it's ready when you get home.'

'Great plan.'

Home.

He looked round at the room decor chosen by Mia. It was their home, not his. Even though he'd helped rebuild it. Even though she'd talked her ideas through with him. Even though he'd helped her choose the paint colours and tiles. He didn't live here, he was always just a visitor sleeping in the spare room so Harper wouldn't get a shock at finding her mother and Brin in bed together. So he wouldn't disrupt their routine or their lives. And he went along with it all because he knew that, after everything she'd endured, Mia craved stability. She saw him as a threat to that.

As he watched her go, his heart contracted. Because the surprise of this whole thing was that, even after his brother had done the unspeakable, Brin did want it all. He wanted the happy-family thing. He wanted Harper to call him Daddy. Now, not later.

Mo stór.

The words fluttered around his chest and he wasn't quite sure if they were meant for Harper or Mia.

They were for both.

Talking to Mia was too easy. But spilling his guts to her had been a weakness. Making love with her was a beautiful, delicious weakness, a weakness that could be exploited. Alarm bells rang loud in his head, gripping his gut and twisting.

He shouldn't be here, doing this.

He should have put a stop to it for both their sakes. And for Harper's too. Because he was doing what he'd promised he'd never do again—he was falling too fast and he couldn't stop it even if he wanted to.

He was pushing the set of drawers back against the wall when his phone rang. Rattled by his realisation, he forced a smile into his voice. How was he going to navigate this? How could he do this and come out whole? 'Mia? Missing me already?'

'Oh, Brin.'

He could tell by her tone and the bubble of breathlessness that something was very wrong. His heart went into freefall. 'What's happened?'

In the background, mingled with the rush of air he could hear a small child crying—his child. Mia sighed. 'Look, don't panic.'

'I'm not panicking.'

He was panicking. His heart rate was skyrocketing, his chest caving. His daughter was crying and he wasn't there with her to stop her tears. It was always going to be like this if they lived so far apart. One of them would always be on the end of the phone in times of need, not there in the heart of it all.

'Tell me, Mia. What's happened?'

She gave a gulp and a stifled sob. 'Harper's had an accident.'

* * *

Mia cradled a still-sobbing Harper to her chest as Carly moored the boat at the harbour.

Brin was standing there, shivering in the dimming daylight, his face a map of worry and fear. He ran forward and took Harper from her. Mia watched him hold his daughter so tenderly, her heart felt bruised. This big man and her little miss—the love she felt for him was overwhelming, distracting and too much.

Too much.

She couldn't breathe at the thought of how much damage he could wreak with one callous word, one dark look.

He stared into Harper's blue O'Connor eyes. 'Hey, big girl. What did you do?'

'Ouchy.' Harper whimpered and heaved air into her lungs between shuddering sobs. 'Sore.'

'I think her arm is broken.' Mia tried to stay calm. It was bad enough she was rattled by her feelings for this man but now her daughter was hurting too. If only she could stop hurt, rewind time, right back to the day her family had left to go fishing. Or the day she'd met Brin. Or to a few hours ago, before she'd let Harper go with Carly so she could spend time in bed making love. But there was nothing she could do but live through it and provide comfort for her child. 'She's going to need an X-ray.'

Brin nodded as he rocked Harper in his arms. 'Tell me again, slowly, what happened?'

'She was riding Mason's little push-along tricycle and fell off at an awkward angle. It happens. Kids fall. It's part of growing up.'

'Should I call for a medical evacuation?' His jaw clenched and she felt a rail of judgement from his black look.

'For a broken arm? It's not that bad, Brin. They won't come for that. We have to get the ferry over to the city.'

'But she's—'

'Your daughter, and she's hurting, I know. They won't send a helicopter for this.'

'They sent one for an electrical injury.' He strode towards her house with his daughter in his arms and she had to run to keep up with him.

'We both know that could have had serious consequences. Nikau's heart needed monitoring. This is a broken arm. It could possibly even wait until morning.'

'No way. We go now.' His eyes shot sparks. 'I'll get my bag. Pack something for her and I'll take her to the hospital. Don't forget her blankie.'

Mia's heart buckled. Things were unravelling; she could see that. They weren't close enough yet and didn't have the longevity to weather a storm like this. She didn't want to have to explain to him that he didn't know what vaccinations Harper had had, or her medical history, and possibly didn't have her date of birth imprinted in his head. He probably didn't know their actual postal address. Besides, she was Harper's mother, and there was no way her daughter was going to hospital without her. 'I'm coming too. We'll get the last ferry over.'

As he threw things into a holdall, he didn't let up. 'This is ridiculous. If you lived on the mainland it'd take a fraction of the time to get her to hospital. She's in pain.'

'I know. And this is the best we can do.'

'It's so far away from anywhere.'

'That's why I love it.'

'So far away from me. All this weekend visiting—it's not enough.' He looked at her then, for a long time, and she felt the implications ripple through her. He needed more from them and he couldn't ask. 'And from the hospital,' he added.

But she couldn't give any more and put her heart on the line. 'This is the first time we've needed the hospital in her whole life.'

'It may not be the last.'

'No, but we can't wrap her in cotton wool, Brin. I've lived on the island my whole life. Many hundreds, if not thousands, still do, and we cope. We get through.'

'I don't want my daughter to cope. I want her to thrive.'

'She *is* thriving.' But she looked down at Harper, who was now lying on the sofa, at her shocked little face and her tear-stained cheeks, and Mia's heart broke. They'd always managed on the island. They were strong and resilient people. He didn't understand. He didn't want to.

The argument abated while they sat in the waiting room, surrounded by other people, and while Harper's X-ray confirmed a fracture. And even while the back slab was applied. They both focused on making their little girl smile, trying to distract her from the pain.

Trying to distract themselves from their own pain too.

'Mumma…' Harper sobbed after the back slab was finished, and put her good arm out to be picked up. Mia swept her up and held her close, stroking her hair.

But then came a restless wriggle, a grouchy face and, 'Bwin.'

She put out her arm again. Her chest was heaving and she made the little sniffling sounds of an exhausted child in pain. Mia's heart broke into tiny pieces. Nothing could calm her daughter. Nothing could soothe her, not even a game of hide-and-seek behind the blankie. Brin tried and tried, but failed to bring a glimmer of a smile.

That *always* worked.

'We need to get her home.' His tone was desperate. 'She needs some rest.'

Home.

Yes. Back to Rāwhiti. Mia didn't say it, she just nodded, because she knew he meant his place. Two parents. Two homes. Two lives.

And now two adults in stony silence on the drive back *home*.

It wasn't until dawn, when Harper was finally asleep in her room at Daddy's house, clutching her beloved blankie in her good hand, that he said the words that ricocheted through Mia's heart. 'I want you to move here. So we can be closer. It makes sense.'

'Not to me.' It had been a long and worrying night and exhaustion nipped at Mia's nerves. She beckoned him out of the room so Harper wouldn't wake to see the two grown-ups upset with each other. When they got to the lounge, she took a deep breath. 'I am not moving, Brin. Rāwhiti is my home. It is my everything.'

Only hours ago she'd thought *he* was. And he was… Oh, even now she ached to be held by him. For them to put this difficult conversation behind them and climb into bed together. But her heart was a shabby, soft, old thing that had been badly bruised. It leapt at any kind of affection, like a little excitable puppy. She wasn't young any more. She couldn't let her heart lead her down that path.

She loved him, but she could not let that be her downfall.

She had to let her head rule. Rāwhiti Island was her place, her life. It was where she'd grown up, where she'd lived with her family. That made sense, to her at least. He couldn't make her do it. She'd already sold her family home; she had to keep their memories alive, keep tethered to them by geography, keep them tied to the people who'd known them. And make sure that Harper got to know and love her heritage too. 'I can't leave. You knew that coming into this.'

He shook his head as he leaned back against the windowsill. 'I didn't know a lot coming into this, Mia. I came for a job and ended up with a family.'

True, he hadn't asked for this. But she knew how much he loved being with them. And how much she loved being part of this family of three. Oh, it was what she wanted. But how could she make it happen and then wait…*wait*…for it all to fall apart? How could she live through that torment, waiting for everything she loved to be lost? 'Is that what you want? A family?'

'I…' He swallowed and looked away. He'd had one before and it had broken him.

'Because, if that's what you really want, why don't you move to Rāwhiti?' The words slipped out of her mouth as a sudden flicker of hope slid under her rib cage. Maybe they could both override their fears. Maybe it could work. Love could find a way on her little island. Love could blossom there.

But his expression was utter sadness. 'You

know that's impossible. My job isn't on Rāwhiti, it's in the city.'

'And you've already given up your life dreams for one family, right?' Why would he risk that again?

His jaw tightened and he turned away.

It was hopeless.

They'd avoided this conversation for too long. They'd hidden behind kisses and long lazy nights, behind getting to know each other in so many ways. Pretended they could do the impossible.

But she couldn't do it. And neither could he. 'I can't move here, Brin. This is not me. And I can't leave them.'

He turned back to look at her. 'They will get another nurse. They have Owen and Carly.'

I can't leave them.

He didn't understand. She was tied to the island inextricably. She couldn't just move away. 'They have me.'

'And I don't.' He turned away to look at the night.

City lights danced outside like glow worms and fireflies. She guessed that once upon a time she might have found it pleasing. Now she wanted to be back home.

He huffed out a breath. 'What would I do on Rāwhiti? I'm a paramedic. I'm based here. There is no paramedic service where you live. I can't just find a job there or make one up.'

'You could try. You know how much that place means to me.'

He walked across the room and ran his fingers along her arm, softly and tenderly. 'I told you before, you bring your family with you in your heart and in your memories. In your stories. We can't stay stuck in one place because of the people we loved there.'

She'd sold their memory and had got a nice new kitchen instead. She damned well would stay there to make sure they weren't forgotten. 'All I have left is a bench with their names on.'

'Bring that too. We'll find you a place with a garden. You know how much you and Harper mean to me.'

'I know you love your daughter.' But her? How did she fit into this for him?

He was suggesting they find a nice place for her and Harper to live on the mainland, not to live with him. Was he saying all this because he wanted Harper in his life with a convenient side serving of Mia? Did his picture of a family even include her? Did he even want a partner? Did he not trust her even now, after everything they'd done and said?

They'd both been alone and independent so long that when things started to get difficult they didn't know how to weather it together. They were too scared, too scarred, to be utterly vulnerable and make a leap.

And she couldn't say, 'I love you,' to him now. She couldn't tell him because that would smack of desperation or coercion. She had to step away before she made a fool of herself.

Her heart broke at the thought of losing him, but she had to do what was best for her family. Her little family of two, the way it had always been. She fisted away tears and dug deep for some courage.

'I'm here, Mia.' But he didn't double down on how much he cared. And he certainly didn't say he loved her.

'For Harper? Or for me?'

'For Harper, of course, and...' He visibly shook and stepped back. 'Mia, I had it all once. I gave everything up for it. Then I lost it.' His tone was raw and low, his breath shaky. 'I don't know... What if...?'

'You don't know if you can give everything up again—your job, your life—for someone who might decide they don't want you. Is that right, Brin? No matter what I say now, it won't change your fears for the future. So you won't give up what you've worked hard for. Not for me. Not for any idea of us.' She nodded. Tried to swallow away the pain in her throat. Tried to ignore the hurt ripping through her chest like a knife wound. This was exactly what she hadn't wanted, everything she'd been hoping to avoid. When he nodded, she bit her lip to stop it from trembling. 'Just so you know, I am not your ex.'

He pressed his lips together then breathed out. 'No.'

'But you still don't trust what we have. What we could grow between us on Rāwhiti.' At his silence, she sighed, almost moaned at the sadness of it all, but managed to hold that in. 'Then it's visits every other weekend only on the island, while Harper's so little. You'll have to find somewhere child-friendly to stay. When she's older, she can come stay here.'

She'd miss them both terribly while they bonded together without her. She would be excluded from their own little family. She was inextricably linked to him for ever. For the next few years, she'd be forced to see him every other weekend, and to message him on Harper's behalf. She'd get to share things with him, but not the private, intimate things, the difficult things or the lovely things. Just the mundane drop-off and pick-up details. The reminders of Harper's schedule. She'd have to watch him grow apart from her...perhaps fall in love with another woman. Maybe have another child.

No.

She couldn't bear it.

God. A scream rose in her throat but she forced it down. How had this gone so horribly wrong? Why did it have to hurt so much?

He shook his head. 'Mia, I'm so sorry.'

'Me too.' Because she loved him and this was the price—her heart, her peace, her everything. She got the booby prize, got to sit on the sidelines of his life instead of being in the spotlight of it. She cleared her throat and made to sound as reasonable as possible, because if she broke now she didn't think she'd recover. 'We'll be gone as soon as she wakes up.'

He nodded, his eyes haunted with grief. 'I know.'

Then he turned and left the room.

And she leaned back against the door and finally let the tears fall.

Brin stormed out of the room, unable to control himself any longer. He'd tried to reason with her. He'd listened to her arguments. He'd answered her comebacks with logic. Moving here was the only sensible thing to do. Rāwhiti was magical, he couldn't deny, but it made sense for them to be here. She could get work at the hospital or any of the many GP practices. Harper would have the pick of schools. But Mia was so wedded to that island, she couldn't see past it.

He ignored the swathe of emotions that threatened to overwhelm him. He would not allow them to impinge on this important life decision. He needed to see his daughter regularly—end of. He'd risked too much in the past. Harper would not be like Niamh—collateral damage from a failed relationship. He would not walk that path again, would not allow his daughter to be used as ammunition—she deserved to have two parents in her life. And he would move heaven and earth for that to happen.

But then there was Mia. Beautiful, funny, gorgeous Mia. Stubborn, too. Independent. She'd had to be. Left alone to bring up a child, she'd learnt to fight. And he loved her for it. He loved her vibrancy, her compassion. He loved the way his soul felt brighter, being in her presence.

His heart rattled at that thought. *Loved?* Did he love her?

No.

He was never going to allow that to happen. Care for, yes. Like, yes. Desire, yes. But more than that? His heart quivered at the thought of being so vulnerable.

The sound of a heavy-duty zip being pulled alerted him to her packing. He couldn't sit here in the bedroom and listen to her prepare to leave, so he grabbed his running gear and headed outside into the marmalade sunrise. Harper was still fast asleep. He had a while before they'd go.

Auckland had fifty-two volcanoes and it felt as if he pushed himself to the top of each one of them, trying to exorcise every feeling he had for Mia. To rid himself of the sweet, sweet memories and the fierce attraction.

His feet hit the tarmac over and over, a rhythm that soothed him a little. Maybe she'd rethink. Maybe they could sit down and chat over breakfast. Maybe…

When he rounded the corner towards his apartment, he saw Mia bending at the back door of a taxi, no doubt clipping Harper into a car seat. His heart lurched. He couldn't believe this was where they'd ended up. They were leaving and his whole world was folding in.

No.

'Wait!'

He raced forward as Mia straightened with such sadness in her eyes, it made his gut hurt.

'We were waiting for you.' Her voice was almost a whisper and her eyes glistened. 'To say goodbye.'

His gut hollowed out. He wanted to reach for her, to pull her against him, to kiss her and hold her. To tell her everything was going to be okay.

It's okay. It's okay. It's okay.

But it wasn't. He'd held back his emotions in the early hours but now they threatened to engulf him. He felt loss, dread, fear. A powerful love for his daughter. Something…*what?*…for Mia. So much, too much, that it clouded his reasoning.

'Bwin.'

He tore his gaze away from Mia to see his little angel, clutching her blankie to her cheek the way she did when she was self-soothing, tired or in pain. Her sleepy smile hit him square in the chest.

'Hey, baby girl.' He stroked her hair. 'You be good for Mumma, okay?'

'Yes.' His daughter blinked up at him and raised her broken arm. 'Ouchy.'

'Yes...' He tried for words, but his throat was blocked. In desperation, he turned back to Mia.

Her lips were pressed together but she nodded and swallowed. 'Bye, then.'

Don't go. It'll be okay.

But it wouldn't. Nothing would be okay again.

She climbed into the front of the car and closed the door, and it felt as if she'd closed off his life-line.

The car started to pull away.

'Harper! Daddy loves you!' he shouted. She couldn't hear him so he blew a kiss, and she copied, her mouth moving, saying something only Mia could hear.

Mia turned then. His Mia. *Mo stór. My darling Mia.*

And her dark gaze latched on to his. He caught a glimpse of the swift swipe of her sleeve across her cheek. Then the car disappeared round the corner.

It was happening again. The two people he cared the most for in the whole damned world would be carving a life without him.

'No!' He raced after the car, wanting to…wanting to what?

Wanting them here, with him. Wanting to clutch them tight to his chest. To grow old with them, to nurture them.

Wanting Mia to be in his life. To *be* his life.

But, shredded on the inside, he watched them go. Because he knew it couldn't happen. He'd learnt that over and over from his father, his brother, his ex.

Love didn't grow where Brin was. Only pain.

CHAPTER FIFTEEN

'So, I HAVE NEWS.' Carly beamed as she wandered into the staff lunch-room.

'You're pregnant?' Mia's eyes strayed from her sad-looking sandwich to Carly's flat belly and she felt a twinge of envy. Again. She could not be jealous of her best friend's happiness. Just because love was not on Mia's cards, it was lovely to have it in her friend's life.

But Carly's smile grew as she shook her head. 'No.'

'Then, what?'

'The new owner of the camp sent an email through asking about a few things and said she's going to turn the place into a wellness centre.'

'Oh? All yoga retreats and açai smoothies?' Perhaps Mia should have been more excited about this. But, truth was, she hadn't felt excited about anything for days, not since she'd left Brin's place almost a week ago. She was listless and empty—broken, in fact. Oh, sure, she was managing to put up a great front, so no one knew. But at night she gave in to the emotions and let her body sob out its loneliness.

She missed him. Missed what they'd had and what could have been.

Carly was still grinning. 'And meditation and mindfulness.'

'Sign me up,' Mia quipped. 'I could do with some quiet time.' Although, being alone with her thoughts was probably not such a great idea. Maybe she needed to be somewhere busy, vibrant, exciting, with a hum of white noise.

Like the city?

Like Brin's apartment?

No. It was all too late to think about that.

'Me too.' Carly sat down across the table from her. 'I would love a massage and some time out.'

'We should book a slot, then, as soon as it opens.' Mia could imagine the resort, with a spa and high-end apartments. It would bring much-needed dollars to the island but wasn't exactly how her parents had envisioned the camp turning out.

'But get this,' Carly added. 'She's also going to donate six weeks a year to Women's Refuge and host victims of abuse here to help them heal— for free. She wants to upgrade the playground, not tear it down. And she's keeping some of the bunk rooms so she can bring children, too, and turn the rest into higher-end accommodation to fund it all.'

'Oh?' Mia's chest felt suddenly a little clearer. 'So, not flash apartments, like we'd heard?'

'No. The real-estate guy had got the wrong end of the stick.'

Mia found herself smiling for the first time in days. 'I know it's none of my business what happens to it, but I'm thrilled it's not going to be a big resort. And helping charities too…that's great.'

Her friend nodded. 'I know you were feeling guilty—I have to admit, I was too. I didn't want you to think I was all about taking Rafferty's money.'

'I would never think that about you. You were my brother's wife. We all loved you.' A rogue tear slipped down Mia's cheek. She scrubbed it away. These days, tears were only a heartbeat away. She felt so sensitive, acutely reacting to every and any emotion.

Carly frowned and slid her hand over Mia's. 'Hey, I didn't realise you were so upset about selling the place.'

'I'm all kinds of confused, to be honest. I needed the money for a better life for Harper, and I can't do that without selling the camp. But I'm so glad it's going to help people too. Mum would have liked that. Dad too.' Mia's throat was scratchy and raw and she wasn't sure she was coping well, holding everything in the way she usually did. She took a deep breath. 'It's not just that. I…um…'

'What is it?'

Mia's brief happiness and relief took a nose-dive. 'Brin.'

'I thought you were getting along. It seemed that way last time I saw you together.'

'Not any more.' Mia filled her in on the details of her last trip to the mainland. 'But he messages every day and tries to say goodnight to Harper every night when he can.'

Carly's eyes brightened. 'That's good, isn't it? He's a good dad. As much as he can be, from a distance.'

'I miss him.'

I love him.

It didn't appear that feeling would abate any time soon. Her treacherous bottom lip started to wobble. She pressed her lips together and willed herself not to cry.

'Oh, honey. Come here.' Carly pulled her into a hug, which made Mia feel even worse.

She tugged away. 'Stop being nice to me or I'm going to cry even harder.'

'Oh, Mia. I'm so sorry.'

'Me too.' Mia sniffed. 'I'm just going to have to be strong for me and Harper.'

Carly brushed soggy strands of hair from Mia's face. 'You are the strongest woman I've ever met. You'll get through this. You've got through worse.'

But this was a different kind of loss. A lifetime wouldn't erase the way she felt about Brin. 'I don't ever want to be in another relationship. It hurts too much.'

'After what happened to Rafferty, I used to think that too, but sometimes you've got to take the risk.' Carly handed her a tissue.

Mia blew her nose. 'I don't like taking risks.'

Carly gave her a curious but sympathetic look. 'You really wouldn't consider moving there to be with him?'

'How can you say that? Rafferty's here.' In fact, Rafferty's body had never been found. They didn't know where he was, or her mother. Her father's body had washed up on a neighbouring island. But there was something symbolic, almost sacred, about Rāwhiti, the place they'd made their home. 'You're not going to leave.'

'I was about to leave when we sold the camp, right? I came back for Owen and Mason, not just for Rāwhiti. But who knows what the future holds? Seriously, if we decided as a family that somewhere else was better for us, I'd go in a heartbeat. It would be an adventure. I met Rafferty travelling, after all. I never intended to live my whole life here.' Her friend's smile was soft and tender. 'Love is in your heart, Mia. It's not a place. You carry your family with you. If you lived on the mainland, you wouldn't forget this island. You'd visit. You'd keep the memories alive. Your family would not want you to be stuck here.'

Those last words had Mia blinking and sitting up. Was she stuck?

Was she using her past to glue her to the island when she should be teaching her daughter to move forward? To embrace new things and not to be afraid of change? A strange sensation slid into her chest. Was she *hiding* behind her lost family and community because she didn't want to take a risk with Brin?

Ouch.

Carly took a deep breath. 'Let me ask you a question, Mia. If Brin moved here would you want to be with him?'

'Of course. I think… Oh, I think I might have fallen in love with him.'

'Oh, trust me, we all know how much you care for him. We can see it. And how much he cares for you too. You're perfect for each other.' Carly squeezed her hand.

'But he wasn't willing to take that step either.' Mia sighed. Because he'd lived through a nightmare. Because she hadn't been willing to discuss their future unless it had been entirely on her terms and he'd respected that. 'I think we're both scared.'

Carly nodded. 'I was terrified of falling for Owen. But doing something scary is life-affirming. Perhaps it's time *you* took that risk, eh? You can't spend the rest of your life hiding here, trying not to care about people. You've got to live,

Mia, in your family's memory. And to show Harper how to be a strong woman. You don't want her afraid to take risks, do you? You want her to be open and curious and willing to reach out, to stretch and grow.'

'I can grow here.' But Mia knew her friend was right. She needed to live her life to the full, not endure a half-life here, being scared and hiding away. She didn't want to be scared any more. She wanted to be the open-hearted woman she'd once been, before her family had been lost to the sea.

She needed to take risks, even if the biggest threat was to her heart. Because love was worth it. Brin was worth it. Their future as a family sure as hell was worth it.

She just had to work out how to convince him to believe it too.

'You're very quiet, Brin. You okay?' Lewis balled the paper bag that had held his sausage roll and threw it into the beach rubbish bin like a basketball player. Then he whooped. 'Slam dunk. Three points to me.'

It was the last hours of a gruelling nightshift, and they were taking a very late break and grabbing some much-needed sunshine and sustenance. But every time Brin set foot on the beach he looked out towards the little islands on the hazy horizon and his heart felt crushed. Mia and Harper were out there. He was here.

'Grand,' Brin answered. Although nothing was grand these days. Sure, he had a daily update on Harper, via Mia's short messages. But he was missing out—not just on watching his daughter grow but on Mia time.

Ever since she'd left his senses had been on high alert, trying to find some fragment of her scent, or her presence in his house.

House. Yes, because it wasn't a home. It was a holding pen until he could find something that would work better for Harper and him. And, even though he had contact with Mia, nothing between them was the same. It was brittle, loaded and broken.

His gut tightened at the thought. At what they'd shared together and now lost.

Jeez, he missed her.

'Okay.' Lewis jumped up and shook his head, brushing sand off his trousers. 'Got to get the van back to base, then I'm out of here. I've got to be at St Joseph's before ten o'clock.'

'St Joseph's?'

'Primary school. My niece is getting an award and they're having a special assembly this morning. If I don't get there in time, my brother will kill me.' Lewis grinned as they walked towards the car park. 'Don't want to be Bad Uncle Lewis. Again.'

'Again?'

'Oh, you know how it is. I missed the Christmas play because I was working. I missed Christmas Day because I was working.'

'Sometimes shift work sucks. You and your brother close?' Brin wondered how it felt to not hate your sibling with as much passion as Brin did. How it felt to see your niece on a regular basis. To have a family that loved each other.

'Twins. Tied at the hip.' Lewis shrugged. 'Any plans for your days off? Please tell me it's something more exciting than a special assembly.'

Brin couldn't think of anything better. Except a long, lazy night with Mia. 'Going to Rāwhiti.'

'To see Mia? Things getting hot there?' His boss's grin was suggestive and teasing.

But Brin's jaw set. Things were very definitely cold. 'It's autumn. Things are cooling a bit.'

Lewis laughed. 'I mean between you and Mia. You seem very close.'

Brin took a deep breath and looked his boss straight in the eye. 'I'm Harper's father. I try to see her when I can.' It was time to tell people. He wanted to scream to the world that he was that cute little kid's daddy.

Lewis's eyes grew wide. 'Whoa, wait, what? You and Mia?'

'Long story. And I'm not going to go there. But, yeah. Three years ago.'

Three years and he'd missed her every damned day. That was after one night. Now he'd had many amazing nights and many glorious days with her, he wasn't sure if his heart was ever going to recover.

He missed her smile, her laugh, her temper. He missed the chats they had after making love, missed holding her, sharing their lives, sharing Harper.

Jeez, he missed everything. He'd loved every minute of being with her.

That word again: love. It kept popping into his head, sliding under his rib cage. Love for Harper, yes, but a different kind of feeling for Mia. An ache that would never stop.

And there wasn't a damned thing he could do about it. Apart from face her, smile and pretend he was okay. 'So I'm going to be requesting regular weekends off. Don't want to be Bad Daddy. Right?'

Daddy. He was going to tell Harper as soon as he thought the time was right. No waiting for Mia to be ready.

And yet, *damn.*

He wanted her to be ready.

Lewis's eyes were still wide with excitement at Brin's news as they climbed into the ambulance. 'Must be tricky with them being over on Rāwhiti and you in the city.'

'Yup.'

'So, you and Mia…?'

Brin held up his hand. 'I said don't go there.'

'I like Mia.' Lewis gunned the engine and

steered into a gap in traffic. 'She's had a really tough time. But she's a tough cookie. Funny, too. Bet she'd bite your head off if you were late to assembly.'

'No doubt.'

She's mine. Hands off.

Possessiveness curled through him, ugly and raw. He couldn't think of Mia with anyone else. He wanted her. He missed her.

Jeez. Did he love her?

No, he didn't.

Yes, he damned well did. He knew it and had been hiding from it. Hadn't wanted to admit that he'd let himself fall so deep and so hard because the consequences would be devastating.

And they had been. Every minute since she'd left, he'd felt broken into a zillion pieces. He loved the woman and there was nothing he could do about it. She didn't want him, did she? She'd almost said so.

Stupid bloody eejit.

Wait…she'd *almost* said so. But she hadn't actually said it, had she? She'd said, 'Is that what you really want? A family? Why don't you move to Rāwhiti?'

His heart jigged.

Why didn't he?

Because he didn't have a job there. But, when Grainne had fallen pregnant and they'd cancelled their cruise jobs, he'd pivoted and retrained. So, he could do something else, right? The handyman was laid up at the moment. They always needed a first-aider. He could put his hand to something—pull a pint, learn how to sail…invent a job.

He had to do something to make things right. To shift this weight in his chest. More importantly, he needed to talk to Mia—really talk. Put aside what he'd been scared of and talk. He hadn't listened. He hadn't *heard* her. She'd never said she didn't want him, she didn't want to be forced to move. And why should she? She'd lived on that island her whole life. Why would she move her daughter's and her whole lives for him just because he'd been too damaged by betrayal to step into something that could be amazing?

He turned to his boss as they pulled into the station. 'Look, Lewis, I know I've just joined the service again, but I might need to leave. In fact, yes. I need to hand in my notice. Now.'

'What?' Lewis's mouth hung open.

'You're right, it's hard being away from them. I need to be on Rāwhiti. With my girls.' *My girls.*

Maybe…surely…they could make it work? The pieces of his splintered heart started to fit themselves back together as hope suffused his chest.

Lewis blinked. 'That's a huge call, Brin.'

'Yeah, I know. And it's about time I made it.'

Mia stood at the ferry terminal and watched the boat dock. Time was her heart would have danced at the thought of seeing Brin disembark. But he wasn't due for his parental visit until later in the week.

So, she was going to see him. A surprise. She hoped it would be a good one.

The last ferry from the mainland was always busy with people returning from city trips so she waited until the crowd had subsided before stepping forward to hand over her ticket to the deck hand.

'Mia?'

She froze at the sound of that voice—deep, warm and, even in such a short word, with a hint of an Irish accent.

She turned to see Brin striding towards her with a holdall slung over his shoulder.

'Brin?' Was she dreaming? What the hell? She ached to run towards him, but she anchored her feet firmly to the ground. Had he come to see her or Harper? Hope rose in her chest but she squashed it. This was how it was always going to be—her heart dancing at seeing him and then the swift realisation that he was not here for her. 'It's not your day until Friday.'

He nodded. 'My plans have changed.'

'Your roster?' Of course. A thick weight crushed her chest. 'You should have said.'

Close up, he looked nervous, tired. 'Mia, I needed to see you.'

'Me?' Her heart hammered hard against her chest wall.

The roar of an engine had him looking behind as the ferry started to glide away from the dock. 'You're missing the ferry. Where are you going?'

'To find you.'

His expression darkened to worry. 'Why? Has something happened? Why didn't you call?'

'I wanted to see you in person. I need to tell you, Brin. I'm sorry we left. I should have stayed and talked some more.'

He shook his head and walked towards the marina, where it was quiet. 'We were all out of talking, I think. We were tired and stressed out.'

Did he understand what she was alluding to? 'No. I mean I should have stayed. With you. But...' Courage slipped away, but she grabbed it. 'I was scared of losing you, scared that if I allowed myself to fall for you it could all be snatched away. One day you might not come home.'

He was still frowning but it had changed into confusion and tenderness. He reached and cupped her cheek. 'Hey, nothing's going to happen to me. But, even if it did, then you'd still have my love. Alive or dead, you'd still have me, Mia. Totally, wholly.'

Mia swallowed. Was she hearing him correctly? 'You love me?'

He chuckled. 'Is it possible to love someone

so fiercely, even if it's the first time you've met them? I mean, that was how you felt about Harper when you birthed her.'

'Yes, of course, but she's my baby.'

'*Our* baby. And it was exactly how I felt about you. Not love at first sight…but maybe.' He laughed. 'You fell into me, and I was all paramedic, assessing you quietly to make sure you were okay. But, really I was trying to catch my breath. You blew me away from that moment. And that night, talking, making love, my heart was yours—always and only yours. I've loved you fiercely since that day, Mia, and I love you even more each day. And the force of it all and what I could lose, how much risk there was… It scared me. I didn't want to lean into it, I wanted to run.'

'But I ran instead.' She couldn't quite believe this was happening. Tears pricked her eyes and this time they were happy tears and sad tears all mingled together. She should have stayed with him. But he was here now. He'd come for her.

He stroked her arm. 'I've been running from a broken family that doesn't love me, but why should I let that colour what I could have? *This* family. I love Harper, obviously. But I *love* you, Mia.'

He loved her. She scrubbed away the tears. 'And I love you, Brin. I was coming to tell you. We'll come to the city and live there. We'll grow something new and good between us. My home isn't here with ghosts and memories. My home is with you.'

'Ah.' His eyes narrowed. 'I've handed in my notice. I'm coming to live here.'

She blinked up at him. 'You did what?'

He nodded definitively. 'I'm leaving my job. I'm going to come and live here, where you want to be.'

'And do what? You're a paramedic.'

He shrugged. 'I'll find something.'

'I don't want you to just find something. That's not what love is. I want you to be fulfilled in your job and your life. I want you to be happy.' She put her hand on his chest. 'So maybe we could do both? Work in the city and visit here at weekends. We've got my house here…it could be our holiday home. And we have your place in the city.'

'Our place in the city. For you, me and Harper. Our family.' He tilted up her chin. 'Any home with you sounds perfect.'

She laughed. 'You are perfect.'

'No, you are,' he teased, and wrapped her into his arms. 'Come here. I love you, Mia Edwards.'

'I love you, Brin. So much.' She looked up into his beautiful face and whispered, 'Kiss me.'

And he did.

EPILOGUE

Eight months later...

MIA STOOD IN her Rāwhiti Island bedroom and looked in the full-length mirror at a reflection she'd never believed she'd ever see.

Something old. She ran her fingertips over her mother's precious diamond earrings.

Your little girl's all grown up with a girl of her own. I wish you were here to share this. I miss you. I love you. And Dad and Raff. But I carry you with me in my heart. For ever.

Something new. She sniffed and smiled. No doubt Brin would be very happy with the fancy new lingerie under her gorgeous A-line wedding dress.

Something borrowed. Carly's diamond bracelet hung from her wrist. It had been Mia's parents' wedding gift to Carly all those years ago, so she wore it with pride, and thanks to her friend for her enduring support and love.

Something blue. She put her hand to her belly. She'd only done the test that morning. Two little blue lines explained the nausea…she'd thought it was nerves. But then, she wasn't nervous about marrying this wonderful, caring, handsome man. She slipped the little test into her bag to show him later.

'Mumma! Mumma! Come on.' Harper barrelled into the room, her flower headband at a jaunty angle. Her pretty white dress was slightly creased, but it didn't matter. Life with a toddler was messy and Mia embraced it all. 'Daddy's waiting.'

Daddy.

She couldn't hear it enough. Mia didn't think her heart had ever been so full. She slid her hand into her daughter's and they stepped outside into the sunshine to a chorus of whoops and cheers. It seemed the whole island was there, clapping and laughing.

Even though she lived in Auckland now and worked at a fabulous practice in the city, they spent as much time as possible here. Brin had kept his job as a paramedic and they'd made it work. She had two homes now and she loved them both.

A flotilla of boats followed hers over to the camp. Carly steered, of course. Mia wasn't sure she could handle a boat today. The new owner had jumped at the chance to host a wedding here and had gone a little overboard with the decorating. The jetty was festooned in white chiffon and flowers, a longer aisle than most, but just perfect.

Brin was waiting at the end, so smart in his suit. Her heart almost flew from her chest with happiness, as it did every day whenever she looked at her gorgeous man.

The ceremony took place in the grassy area in front of the beach. Then came a barbecue dinner, dancing and laughter with friends—Anahera, Nicole, Nikau and all the others. *Whanau*: family. Carly, Owen and Mason. Love. So much love.

Later, as they stepped into the honeymoon accommodation in a secluded part of the island, Brin took her in his arms. 'What a wonderful day. You, me and our daughter. A perfect family of three.'

'Ah. About that...' She put her hand on his chest. 'A family of...um...four.'

He frowned. 'What?'

'There's going to be a new addition. Happy wedding, husband.'

'For real? You're pregnant?' At her nod, his eyes grew moist. 'Whoa. And you've just done the conga around the camp. Sit down. What do you need?'

'For a paramedic, you're mighty concerned about a perfectly normal condition.' She laughed. 'I need you. That's all.'

'How did I get this lucky?' He slid his hand over hers, cradling her barely-there bump. 'This time I get to watch you both grow. I love you, Mrs O'Connor.'

'I love you, Brin. More than anything.' She kissed him. 'Together, for ever.'

A family of…four.

* * * * *